"**Mr. Pitborough,**" Cecily cried. "I do not seem able to make myself clear! I am not the only girl in Milchester. There are many others who will be ready to marry you if I am not. Of that I am sure."

"I am sure of it too," Charles Pitborough said with sublime conceit. "But I happen to have fixed my mind upon you as being the one most suitable for my purposes."

"Oh!" she cried, exasperated. "I am afraid you are a very obstinate man."

"I am afraid I am," he agreed.

The moment they reached the hotel Cecily said with some emphasis, "Goodbye, Mr. Pitborough!"

"Good night, Miss Floyd," he said, correcting her, and smiled as he lifted his hat. "I should warn you, perhaps, that I usually get what I want."

Fawcett Crest Books
by Mary Ann Gibbs:

HORATIA

THE ROMANTIC FRENCHMAN

THE GLASS PALACE

THE ADMIRAL'S LADY

A MOST ROMANTIC CITY

A
Most
Romantic
City

Mary Ann Gibbs

A FAWCETT CREST BOOK

Fawcett Publications, Inc., Greenwich, Connecticut

A MOST ROMANTIC CITY

THIS BOOK CONTAINS THE COMPLETE TEXT OF
THE ORIGINAL HARDCOVER EDITION.

A Fawcett Crest Book reprinted by arrangement with
Mason/Charter

ISBN: 0-449-23300-6

Printed in the United States of America

10   9   8   7   6   5   4   3   2   1

A
Most
Romantic
City

1

It was in the January of the first year of the last decade of the century that the Lavenders announced their intention of going abroad in the spring, but it was not until March that their friends learned that in fact they intended going with a Cook's tour. The surprise that was felt was countered nevertheless by the pronouncement of Mrs Blades, wife of the Colonel of the regiment at present occupying Milchester Barracks, that, Cook's tour or not, there was nothing like travel for broadening the mind.

And as Mrs Blades had accompanied her husband to most quarters of the globe during his long career, and therefore must have a mind as broad as Salisbury Plain, it was felt that she knew what she was talking about.

"But my dear Mrs Blades," protested Mrs Floyd, the widowed sister of General Masterson, who had

offered her and her family a home with him in Milchester on the death of her husband five years earlier.
"A *Cook's tour*? Think of the people who go on such
tours—such a very mixed society!"

"On the contrary, some of the best people in the
land travel by Cook's tours," said Mrs Blades in her
downright way. "Mr Lavender will be assured of
having rooms reserved for him in the best hotels, and
of having English food served to him there, and I am
sure he will be particular about that. I do not mean
that unkindly," she continued, because she was a nice
woman. "The Lavenders are worthy, well-meaning
people, and Mr Lavender must feel very much at a
loss now that his son has taken over his share in the
family business. It *is* shipping, I think?"

"Yes," sighed Mrs Floyd, "shipping." Her tone
implied that though it might be a superior trade,
however one looked at it, it was still trade.

"When my husband retires from the Army," said
Mrs Blades firmly, "I shall make him look about at
once for a small country estate to keep him occupied.
Preferably one with a home farm. Nothing keeps an
Englishman more contented than thinking he is a
farmer."

Mrs Floyd could not imagine Mr Lavender looking about him for a country estate, small or large,
while as for having a farm she doubted if he knew
a cow from a pig. A short fat man, looking vaguely
uncomfortable in country tweeds, with a solid gold
hunter at the end of a solid gold chain stretched across
a too solid waistcoat, he never seemed to be entirely
separated from the City of London where his business
was situated. He admitted that he had bought his

house in Milchester because there was such an excellent train service, thus enabling him to keep his finger on the pulse, though whether the pulse in question belonged to his son or to his business or to the City of London he did not explain.

"I understand they are taking Rosalind with them," went on Mrs Blades in a satisfied voice. The Lavenders' only daughter was the prettiest girl in Milchester and had caused havoc among the young officers at the Barracks, a fact of which Miss Lavender was fully aware. "Are there any more young people going?"

"A cousin, I believe," said Mrs Floyd distantly. She would not have had it thought that she was on terms of any great intimacy with the worthy and well-meaning Lavenders, although her eldest girl, Cecily, was a friend of Rosalind's. "It is not an expedition I should fancy, and as for your remark about the best hotels, Mrs Blades, I understand that Mrs Lavender has been advised to take Keating's Powder with her for"—she dropped her voice—"*bugs!*"

"Oh, that is nothing!" The Colonel's lady laughed. "The standards of some of the best hotels abroad may be far below that of our own. I have never travelled without Keating's, and some of my friends swear by Kalydor—and then there is oil of almonds, which is essential for warding off mosquities. Bed bugs are not the worst insects that you meet abroad, Mrs Floyd. Sometimes when I was in India and my mosquito netting was faulty I could not see out of my eyes by the morning."

"Oh dear!" Mrs Floyd shuddered. She had very pretty eyes. "One can understand such things in those parts, Mrs Blades, but one would have thought that countries in Europe would be cleaner."

"Not quite such a high notion of cleanliness as we have in England, I'm afraid," said Mrs Blades.

"*Foreigners!*" said Mrs Floyd. She was glad she was not Mrs Lavender. "I understand they intend to keep with the tour as far as Switzerland, but after that they go on to Italy on their own."

"Yes. Mrs Lavender told my husband that the tour would include Paris, where he wishes to look up a business friend, and they part company with Thomas Cook at Lucerne. I believe Mr Ferndean is to join them there. He would have liked to accompany them to Italy but he could not spare the time."

"Ah!" Mrs Floyd's tone was significant. "Poor Mr Ferndean!"

"I don't know why you should say that. I should have put him down as a very fortunate young man. His father in Parliament, his mother related to some of the nobility, he himself a rising young barrister, with every prospect of making a name for himself in the profession he has chosen. No, I do not think Giles Ferndean is any object of pity."

"I was thinking of Rosalind Lavender," said the widow acidly. "He has proposed to her several times, so I have heard, and she has steadily refused him. Her parents are most upset about it."

"I don't wonder. His breeding and her money would have made a very good match of it." Mrs Blades laughed. "Perhaps that is why he is joining them in Switzerland—in the hope that the romantic Alps will encourage her to change her mind!"

Mrs Floyd agreed without a great deal of enthusiasm. She regarded Rosalind Lavender as a spoilt young woman and she wished that her poor Cecily had such a desirable young man as an admirer. But alas, Cecily had no admirers at all, which her mother regretfully considered to be not surprising, as her daughter's looks were not in the same class as Rosalind's. Neither were they, for that matter, in the same class as her own. Mrs Floyd was a fair, fluffy little woman and she often told her daughter that when she had been Rosalind's age she had been a great deal prettier.

Cecily took after her uncle, General Masterson: her features were fine, her pale face clear-cut, her eyes a warm hazel. But there was no curl to her dark hair and she resolutely refused to put her thick fringe into curlers at night, or to use her mother's curling tongs on it by day. She was a clever girl, and although she might not shine in company, preferring to hold her tongue and listen to others, she was also extremely good-natured, acting as a governess to her younger sister Bella when Miss Cooper was not there. She took her to and from her music and dancing lessons, and spent her spare time in hearing spelling and scales, besides mending her brothers' clothes and sewing on their buttons, which they appeared to wrench off almost as soon as she had put them on.

She was always ready to act as lady's maid to her mother too, dressing her hair for her and cheerfully having her cast-off dresses altered to fit herself.

Yes, thought Mrs Floyd on that March afternoon, as she made her way home from Quebec Street where Colonel Blades' house was situated, Cecily was a good and useful daughter to her. She was not likely to marry, or to make a good match if she did: it was

little Bella who would do that when she grew up—
little fair-haired Bella who had inherited her own looks
and love for clothes. Whereas probably Cecily would
select a penniless curate for a husband because she
was sorry for him.

The sun was sinking behind the trees as she reached
Tilverton Park: she did not hurry, and as she strolled
along she saw her two daughters ahead of her and
remembered that it was the afternoon for Bella's
dancing class. She called after them and they turned
and waited for her to join them, Bella giggling over
something that had happened that afternoon.

"Well, you two," Mrs Floyd said, looking fondly
at her younger daughter as she spoke. "Are you not
going to tell me what you are laughing at?"

"It was Mr Pitborough," Bella said, with a hop,
skip and a jump. "He came to fetch Janie again and
one of the girls whispered to me while we were getting
on our wraps to go home that she thought he must
be sweet on Miss Pert!"

"The dancing mistress?" Mrs Floyd was shocked.
"Bella, whatever put such a vulgar idea into the child's
head?"

"I don't know," said Bella with a fresh burst of
giggles. "But it is the third time he has called for
Janie lately, and I am sure he is not interested in her
dancing, because he never comes into the Assembly
Rooms, and anyway she bounces about like a rubber
ball!"

"I don't think it is very nice to talk about little
Janie Pitborough like that, dear," said her mother,
but she was smiling as Bella ran on happily ahead.
"Do you know why Mr Pitborough is so interested

in Janie's dancing class all at once?" she asked her elder daughter.

Cecily took her time to reply. Her usually pale face was slightly flushed as she said that Mr Pitborough was not likely to confide any reasons he might have to her. "He is not a man I admire," she added, "but I have never seen him address two words to Miss Pert—nor in fact to anyone else. He never speaks to anyone."

"He is very rich," said her mother. "And rich men do some peculiar things at times. But Miss Pert—no!" The dancing mistress with her fading charms, her black silk skirts lifted to show the class her pointed toes in their beaded slippers, placed in the first position, her affected manner and her shrill voice—"One—ah—two—ah—three—Now all together!" was certainly not likely to attract a man like Charles Pitborough.

When his wife died some years previously all the Milchester ladies with unmarried daughters had been very compassionate towards him, many of them feeling that his house Oatesby Hall, three miles outside the town, was in urgent need of a new mistress, and little Janie, then aged two, in need of a mamma. Unfortunately Mr Pitborough did not appear to share that view. His aunt, Miss Hannah Pitborough, had come to keep house for him after his wife's death and was still there, while Janie was looked after by an old, stout nurse, Mrs Appleby, under whose strict ministrations she seemed to bloom. A revulsion of feeling then set in, the ladies declaring that he was a selfish monster of a man, with no thought of making a cheerful home for his little girl.

The Bishop's wife and Mrs Blades continued to ask him to their dinner parties, however: the Colonel's wife said that she was sorry for the poor man, Miss Pitborough's sour face being enough to turn the cream on the trifle, while the Bishop's wife said that we must be charitable to our neighbors, mustn't we?

Cecily disliked the man with good reason; in fact, ever since the New Year's ball at the Bishop's Palace. She had worn her only evening dress for the occasion, a white one made of muslin from her schoolroom days coupled with a *mousseline de soie* of her mother's.

She was so much taller than Mrs Floyd that one dress would not have done, however skilfully their dressmaker, little Miss Kemp, had altered it. So the bodice of the muslin was cut square in the neck and the sleeves were shortened to elbow length, and the skirt and train of the other dress had been added, and Mrs Floyd declared that by the time Miss Kemp had finished nobody would have known that it was not a new dress.

Cecily felt this to be an exaggeration, especially as it had been difficult to hide a stain on the skirt where her mother had spilt some champagne, but as she had no money to buy material for a new one she added some green ribbons on her own account, and the amber necklace that the General had given her on her twenty-first birthday, and had been quite happy with her second-hand finery until her mother told her later of something she had overheard during the evening.

It was that night after she had helped her to get out of her dress and was starting to do up her fringe in curlers in place of the lady's maid that she could not now afford that Mrs Floyd said plaintively:

"I do wish, dear, that you would curl your own hair as well as mine. No wonder people think you are dowdy, with that straight fringe. It is most unbecoming, Cecily."

"Who thinks me dowdy?" asked Cecily, pausing for a moment to find a suitable curling rag for her mother's fringe.

"Of course I know that Miss Kemp does not cut as well as a Court dressmaker," went on Mrs Floyd. "She does not pretend to be more than she is—just a hard-working little country dressmaker. But she is very useful and not expensive, and I did not think your dress looked at all bad considering."

"Who thinks me dowdy?" Cecily repeated, curler in hand.

"Oh, it was only that Mr Pitborough." Mrs Floyd rather wished she had not spoken. "He was standing near me, talking to Mrs Blades, and of course he did not know that I was your mother. Mrs Blades asked him if he were not a dancing man and he said he had not danced for years. So she said he ought to start again, and could she not introduce him to a partner? Well, he looked about him and then he said he would like to meet the tall dowdy girl talking to the Bishop's daughters, and I looked to see who it was he meant, and you may imagine what I felt when I saw it was you!"

Cecily said nothing, but she pulled a piece of hair into a curler too tighly and had to undo it again. "You did dance with him, didn't you, dear?" said her mother.

"I would not have done so if I'd known what he had

said about me," Cecily replied crisply, and rolled up the piece of hair more gently.

"What did he talk about?" asked her mother.

"What does one usually talk about to somebody one does not know at a ball? We were both intent on not treading on each other's feet, but I think I asked him how his daughter was and that he said she was very well, and that she had escaped the influenza epidemic as he and his aunt had. And I said that we had escaped it too, though we have been apprehensive for the boys for a time, as there had been quite a severe outbreak at the Cathedral School. I believe he asked how long we had been in Milchester, and I said five years, and he asked if I liked the town and I said I thought it was very like other cathedral cities, and that was the sum total of our conversation. Oh, and he did apologize once for inadvertently having trodden on my toe. If I had known what you have just told me I might have begged him not to apologize, as the dowdiest girls always get the clumsiest partners."

Mrs Floyd smiled. "The Pitboroughs always have had a lot of money, dear," she said, with a hint of reproof.

"But surely money does not give people the right to be rude about others?" protested Cecily. She had no desire to improve her acquaintance with Mr Pitborough, however, and as her mother did not reply to her question, but only yawned, she finished with her hair, helped to unlace her stays, and slipped her nightdress over her head before hanging up the balldress in the large mahogany wardrobe.

Then she kissed her good night and got herself to bed in the room she shared with Bella, which did not take nearly so long. But for the remainder of that night until she dropped off to sleep, Mr Pitborough's words had come back from time to time to provoke her.

* * * * *

Charles Pitborough was one of four partners in the private bank of Pitborough and Orde, started by his grandfather under the name of Gabriel Pitborough at the end of the eighteenth century. Charles's mother had been an Orde and after her husband's death she had met an attractive American while on a visit to New York with her brother Herbert and shortly afterwards she had married him. She lived now in Boston, visiting Britain once a year to see Janie, and going on to Italy to see her married daughter Miriam and her Italian husband and family. She was fond of Enrico.

Of Charles's three partners in the bank, two were his wealthy Orde uncles, Herbert and Joseph, whose fortunes came originally, as his mother's had, from cotton. They seldom visited the bank, partly because of their still paramount interest in cotton, and partly because they had never forgiven Charles's father, Henry Pitborough, for what they considered to be sharp practice where their sister's fortune was concerned.

Matilda Orde at seventeen had brought Henry sixty thousand pounds as her dowry, and although it was long before the Married Woman's Property Act had come into being, her father had stipulated that Henry was only to use the income from the money, the capital to be held in trust for any children the couple might have. Shortly after his marriage, however, Henry persuaded his wife to sign away thirty thousand to him to invest on his own account, promising to repay it with interest at the end of six months. This promise he kept to the letter, but as he had doubled the money by that time, his brothers-in-law contended that not only had he broken the law in using their sister's capital, but that the whole amount should be added to the existing sixty thousand. Henry Pitborough saw no reason for this: to him it had been a purely business arrangement, and it did not lessen the Ordes' anger when the thirty thousand he had raised in this fashion was used by him to found is own personal fortune, which when he died, amounted to half a million.

The coolness between the Ordes and Pitboroughs, deepened by the cotton famine of the sixties caused by the American Civil War, continued after Henry's death, Joseph preferring to live in Lancashire and not making the journey to Milchester more than once a month—if then—while Herbert spent most of his time abroad in the pursuit of cotton from such distant lands as India, and the bank was fortunate if it saw him once in twelve months.

It was left to the third partner, a Pitborough cousin, William, to attend to the business of the bank with Charles. And as William was addicted to wild-cat schemes where investments were concerned—schemes that his older cousin relentlessly crushed—any important decisions had to be made by Charles himself.

It was perhaps no wonder that Charles, at thirty-five, had developed the air of a much older man, and although Joseph Orde was still the Senior Partner it was his nephew who occupied his room in his absence, and was treated by the staff as the one in authority. It was seldom that he allowed himself the relaxation of an evening party, or the pleasure of fetching his small daughter from her dancing class, and his austerity silenced criticism.

"How many times has Mr Pitborough called for little Janie?" asked Mrs Floyd as she walked across the park with Cecily behind Bella that afternoon.

"Twice or three times perhaps. I really do not know, Mamma." Cecily was bored with Mr Pitborough. "She loves going home in the dog-cart instead of the closed carriage that is usually sent for her and her nurse, and I suppose when the weather is fit and his bank business allows it her father takes her home in it for a treat as he did today. She is a fat little thing, but there is something very taking about her."

Her thoughts went back to that afternoon, and the child's round rosy face and crimped fair hair—her nurse evidently believed relentlessly in making her charge's hair curl—thrust under a little fur bonnet with rose-coloured satin ribbons.

The dancing class was held in the Assembly Rooms at the Tilverton Arms Hotel, and a large and chilly bedroom was set aside to accommodate the children's wraps, and while Bella was hunting for her gloves Cecily's attention had been caught by little Janie, who seemed on the verge of bursting into tears of sheer frustration and rage as she struggled with the tiresome business of buttoning a pair of French kid boots.

Cecily had gone to her assistance with the aid of a buttonhook taken from the holland bag that held Bella's dancing sandals, and kneeling down beside her she buttoned up the little boots quickly and efficiently.

"No need for you to trouble yourself, Miss Floyd," said the old nurse crossly. "She won't hold still, and if she is on the wriggle all the time we are twice as long. Now hold your sleeves, miss, while I put your coat on."

"I'm so afraid Papa will go without me," wailed Janie.

"Your papa will go too, if you don't do as I says," said the nurse wrathfully. "Hold your sleeves down, like I said, or else straight to bed when you get home, my lady, without any tea. That's what will be in store for you."

"Supposing I go to the window and see if he is there?" suggested Cecily coaxingly. "You do as Nurse tells you while I look." She went to the window and then wished she had not, as Mr Pitborough chose that moment to come up the hotel steps and looked up and saw her there. She drew back quickly and told Janie that the groom was at the horse's head and that her father had just gone into the hotel, so that it did not look as if he were in any hurry. Janie thereupon submitted to the pulling and pushing that were thrust upon her and forgot her anxiety and, ready at last, took Cecily's hand down the wide staircase, with Bella, her gloves found, on the other side, and the cross old nurse following behind. But directly she saw her father waiting for her the child forgot everything else and ran to him with delight. It was evident that the ride in the dog-cart was a special treat, perhaps for a child to whom treats might be rather rare.

"Did Mr Pitborough see you there today?" asked Mrs Floyd, pursuing some rather obvious thought of her own.

"Oh yes. At least he acknowledged my presence with a stiff bow. We did not speak." Cecily glanced at her mother drolly. "It would take more than a dowdy girl like me to attract a man like Mr Charles Pitborough. He was only being polite, Mamma, in fact he probably took me for Bella's governess."

"Cecily!" Mrs Floyd glanced at her daughter's shabby clothes with a touch of contrition. "It does not matter how you are dressed, dear. Anybody can see that you are a lady."

"Can they? But I should think that most people like Mr Pitborough judge their acquaintances by their clothes and their money."

There was in fact only one thing of which she approved in Charles Pitborough and that was the way in which he treated his small daughter. Tall and thin, with dark hair going grey at the temples, cold watchful grey eyes and an austere manner, he was not the answer to any girl's prayer for a rich, indulgent husband. Rich he might be, but indulgent—never. It was only when he caught the child up in his arms that the austerity vanished and the coldness in his face melted. "Well, Pudding," he said, "you have got the dog-cart you see." The nickname, earned by her round little figure and general plumpness, was an endearment in itself. "It is waiting outside for your ladyship."

"Oh yes." Her eyes went past him to the waiting conveyance with delight. "Will you let me drive?"

"Well, I suggest we both drive, in case White Star turns nervous in the High Street." They went off down the steps with the little girl's hand tucked confidently into his, and Cecily, watching from the doors of the hotel with Bella, saw the groom lift her up beside her father. Then the old nurse was pushed and hauled up on the other side to keep her from rolling off, a rug was tucked round them and they were off, Janie's hands on the reins beneath her father's, as she chattered away like a sparrow. As she watched them go, Cecily had thought of the great house at Oatesby at the end of its avenue of walnut trees, and she had wondered what sort of welcome waited for the litle girl behind its doors. She hoped that it would not be early to bed and no tea.

The ladies in Milchester were not alone in thinking it was time that Charles Pitborough married again. His cousin's wife, Mrs William, was always introducing him to the nicest girls in the county with little success. Her hopes had risen a little at the Palace ball when she had seen him dancing with Cecily.

"It is the first time I have seen Charles dance with anybody since Gussie died," she had told her husband in the carriage going home.

"He soon deserted the ballroom for whist," said William.

"But he did seem to be talking to his partner," said his wife cheerfully.

"And I can guess what they were talking about as well as you can, my love," said William grinning. " 'What a lot of snow we have had this winter, Miss Floyd. Are you not glad it is gone?' And, 'Does your little daughter like snow, Mr Pitborough? Do you think we shall have any more?' No, that cat won't jump. I have seldom seen a man less interested in his partner than Charles was tonight." After a moment he added, "Aunt Hannah was saying the other day that she thought Gussie's behaviour—and death—killed

Charles's interest in women, and after having watched him tonight with Miss Floyd—who is not a fool by any means—I am beginning to think that she is right."

2

Cecily Floyd and Rosalind Lavender lived not far from each other in Tilverton Crescent, a wide residential road on the outskirts of the town.

The former owner of the land that included Tilverton Park and the superior houses that stood in the Crescent facing on to it at the top of the hill, had been the 8th Lord Tilverton, who, seeing factories encroaching every day on the town, and the railway threatening the view from his rather dreary old mansion, had been glad to sell the leasehold to a local builder for development, retiring to Oughton Park, his other estate in the country.

The handsome white houses, built twenty years after the Queen's accession, were now over thirty years old, and each stood in its large garden. They had been intended from the beginning for well-to-do gentlefolk, and although old Lady Scrimgour in the middle, Judge

Kirby at one end and General Masterson at the other might uphold that tradition of gentility, one of Britain's new industrialists, Mr Lavender, had shocked their sensibilities a little at first when he bought No. 12. But when it was discovered that he was a very inoffensive little man, and that his wife was willing to help with bazaars and to give generously to charitable projects in the town, and that his daughter was very pretty, with charming manners, and certainly likely to be an heiress, the family had in a very short while been accepted by the other residents there almost as if Mr. Lavender had been one of themselves.

The Crescent was separated from the park by a pleasant gravelled road. The park still retained many of its old trees and the shrubs that had been planted there had grown up into small wildernesses intersected by winding paths where nurses could take their charges, and where ladies could exercise their dogs.

At the back of the Crescent houses was a little lane, locally known as Love Lane, and used as a service road for tradesmen's carts and for the stables that housed the resident's horses and carriages. At the bottom of this lane there were a few cottages still owned by the present Lord Tilverton and inhabited by some of his old servants, who had married sons and daughters living in Milchester and were employed as gardeners, grooms and coachmen by the owners of the Crescent houses, while their wives took in washing and their unmarried daughters went into service there.

The last cottage in the lane belonged to a Mrs Chadwell, an old dame who had at one time been nurse in Lord Tilverton's family. She did a little plain sewing for Lady Scrimgour sometimes, and she had

been known to undertake nursing for the Judge's wife
when that lady suffered a serious illness, but it was
generally known that Lord Tilverton had pensioned
the old lady off generously allowing her to live in
her cottage rent-free, and she was considered to be
sufficiently independent to make any request for her
services a matter of some delicacy.

One morning in March, when Rosalind Lavender
and Cecily Floyd were taking a morning's walk in
Tilverton Park, Rosalind asked her friend if she had
seen the young man who was staying with Mrs Chadwell.

"I did not even know that a young man was staying
with her," said Cecily.

"First of all it was put about that he was her grandson." Rosalind was eager to tell her about it as they
strolled along. "But I don't think anybody belived that,
because everybody was saying how good-looking he
was." From which Miss Floyd gathered that Rosalind
had been discussing the gentleman in question with
some of her friends. "We were all dying to know why
he should have his arm in a sling, and his head bound
up, and how it was that he spoke like a gentleman."

"My dearest Ros!" Cecily uttered a mild protest.
"I suppose Mrs Chadwell's grandson could speak
like a gentleman, even so?"

"He *could*," agreed Rosalind, but her eyes were
dancing and from the look on her face Cecily guessed
that she probably knew more about the mysterious
guest in Mrs Chadwell's cottage than anyone else in
Milchester. "Papa said he thought one of her grand-
sons had gone into the Royal Navy, and that he
might have risen to be an officer, and perhaps he had

been wounded in a battle. Only he couldn't remember any recent battle in which our Navy had been engaged."

"Neither can I," said Cecily.

"Well, maybe he just slipped on the deck and broke his arm," suggested Rosalind.

"Careless of him," remarked Cecily drily, and then as her friend laughed outright, "I presume you have seen the young man and know all about him? And if so, might one ask where you have met him? A young man purporting to be a grandson of old Mrs Chadwell is not likely to be entertained in Mrs Lavender's drawing-room, nor those of her friends."

Rosalind blushed slightly, "Well," she said, "if you will promise not to tell—"

"That depends on what you have been doing." Cecily was uncompromising.

"I have done nothing!" Rosalind shook her arm impatiently. "And it is entirely for his sake, poor young man, so if you won't promise I can't tell you."

"Very well, I'll promise."

"I was taking Bonnie for a walk, and you know how she will go chasing after squirrels in the park here, and I was tired of calling her. So I took her on down Love Lane, where there are only rabbits and she doesn't chase them. At the bottom of the lane I stopped to pick the first primroses—there are always a few early ones there in March—and Bonnie started barking and I looked up, and there he was, looking at me over Mrs Chadwell's hedge. He had his arm in a sling and a plaster on his head, and do you know who he is?"

"I've not the slightest idea."

"He's Mr Barnaby Tilverton, Lord Tilverton's nephew, the only son of that younger brother of Lord Tilverton's, who was such a bad lot. I recognized him at once, because he was at the Palace ball last winter, and he asked to be introduced to me, and we danced four dances together; which made Papa very angry."

"Why did it make him angry?" Cecily thought that Mr Lavender, who had a great liking for titles, might have been gratified by Barnaby Tilverton's choice.

"Well you see, Barnaby is in Lord Tilverton's black books, and it doesn't look as if he will ever get out of them, because his father, the Honourable Rupert, ran through an entire fortune—gambling and betting and that sort of thing. And when he died Barnaby was only a little boy of ten, and soon afterwards his mother died too."

"But I suppose Lord Tilverton had him to live at Oughton Park, where there were plenty of people to look after him?"

"No, that he didn't. He sent him to Christ's Hospital, because he was one of the governors there, or something of that sort, and he had nowhere to go for the holidays, not even for Christmas, because his uncle wouldn't have him at Oughton. And so he stayed all the time at the school, until he grew too old for it, and then Lord Tilverton obtained a clerk's post for him in a government office, and he has been there ever since."

"Did Mr Tilverton tell you all this over Mrs Chadwell's hedge?"

"Oh no. Then he only said that—he had hoped he would see me again—and that he had been thinking

about me ever since the Palace ball. And I said I'd
been thinking about him too."

"Rosalind! You have been flirting with that unfor-
tunate young man."

"No, I haven't." Rosalind's pretty face was graver
than Cecily had ever seen it. "I would never flirt with
Barnaby—I mean, Mr Tilverton—Cis. He is much
too nice."

"And what about Mr Ferndean?"

"Oh bother Mr Ferndean!" Rosalind dismissed her
brother's friend, who was also her parents' choice of
a future husband for her, with contempt. "The next
time I met Mr. Tilverton—"

"You have not been meeting him regularly, I hope?"

"But I have to take Bonnie for walks, don't I?"
She slipped her hand back into her friend's arm and
gave it a squeeze. "Don't look shocked, Cis. You've no
idea how brutal Lord Tilverton has been to him.
Poor Barnaby—Mr Tilverton, I mean—was in a
hansom cab with a friend when the horse shied and
they were both thrown out. The friend was not hurt,
but Mr Tilverton broke his arm and cut his head
open, and though Lord Tilverton was told about it,
he did not lift one finger to help him. But do you know
who did? Old Mrs Chadwell—whom he calls Chaddy.
She was his nurse long after she had finished being
nurse to Lord Tilverton's children, and she says that
Barnaby was the best of all her babies. He says that
she always calls her charges "her" babies. Directly
she heard about the accident, she went to London by
herself, and she took a cab all the way from Euston
station to his lodgings, and she brought him back here

to her cottage, where she has been looking after him ever since."

"That was very kind of her." Cecily thought that considering the shortness of their acquaintance Rosalind had managed to find out a great deal about young Mr Tilverton.

"He told me that somebody else in Milchester has been very kind to him too," went on Rosalind seriously. "And that is Mr Charles Pitborough. You wouldn't take him for a kind man perhaps?"

"No, I would not," agreed Cecily emphatically.

"It's that stern, cold manner of his, I expect. You see, as long as Barnaby—Mr Tilverton—is ill, he is not paid, and without the miserable salary that the government office pays him he is quite penniless. So he went to see Mr Pitborough to tell him, and to ask him what he should do, because he did not want to be a burden on Mrs Chadwell. And do you know, Mr Pitborough told him that he would allow him to draw cheques on his bank for a certain amount— Mr Tilverton did not tell me how much of course— until he was better again. He thinks he must be the nicest banker in Britain."

"But I daresay Lord Tilverton's account is with Pitborough and Orde's Bank and so Mr Pitborough knew he was quite safe. I mean, he knows he will be repaid for his so-called kindness whenever it becomes necessary." Cecily dismissed Mr Pitborough and his kindness contemptuously. "And how often have you met Mr Tilverton altogether?"

"I'm afraid I've been meeting him every day, but you mustn't say a word, Cis, because if my parents found out they would send me to stay with my aunts in Islington—who are so proper that you'd think they'd been born with pokers down their backs. It is quite true, Cis, and it is nothing to smile about. I'm not allowed to read novels when I'm there, and I have to help entertain their friends, who are as pokerish as themselves. I wish we were not going off on this tour at the end of next month," she added with a small sigh.

"Rosalind, it will be a lovely trip. You know it will. And you will have forgotten all about Mr Tilverton by the time you come back."

"No, I shall not. I shall never forget him. I think I fell in love with him at the Palace ball and I shall love him till I die."

She glanced at Cecily's amused face. "I know I've said such things before, but I mean it this time. You always know when you have met your fate."

Cecily tried not to laugh, but she did not quite succeed and Rosalind looked at her reproachfully. "If we take our walk that way this morning you will see him for yourself," she said. "He is probably waiting for me in the lane."

"Certainly not." Cecily was firm: it was not the first time she had had to curb Rosalind's interest in undesirable young men. "There must be some reason why your father did not wish you to dance with Mr Tilverton. Perhaps he knows that he has inherited some of his father's vices."

"No, it's only because he has no money and because Lord Tilverton does not like him. Papa has a great respect for Lord Tilverton and he would not do anything to offend him for the world." Rosalind shook her head. "It is no good, Cis," she said, her voice trembling a little. "I feel that mine is fated to be a hopeless love." She gave the arm in hers a second impatient shake. "You are smiling again! How can you be so heartless?"

"I am not heartless, my dear, but I really do not think you should allow yourself to be serious over a young man like Mr Tilverton."

"You talk as if I could help falling in love. Have you never been in love, Cis?"

"Never. I've not had time for such luxuries, my dear." Cecily's voice was crisply cool. "And now I must go. It is Mrs Blades' dinner party tonight and I have promised Mamma to go through her dresses with her to see which one is suitable for her to wear."

As she walked home, however, Cecily thought of old Mrs Chadwell's visitor with some uneasiness, and she hoped that Rosalind's stolen meetings with him would not spread abroad. She did not remember having seen him at the Palace ball, but if he was as good-looking as he was said to be it would not be long before all the girls in Milchester came looking for primroses in Love Lane.

The General's house was the smallest in the Crescent, having been selected by him for that reason. He had never married and had been extremely comfortable at No. 40 until his brother-in-law died and he felt himself bound to offer his roof and hospitality to his sister and her four children.

It had not been an easy decision: the lady was given to what her brother described as "the vapours," and to accommodate an additional five people, with enough servants to wait on them in a house that had until then held but himself, his manservant Pringle, who also acted as groom, a housekeeper and two maids, was no small task. Moreover, ever since she had been there Mrs Floyd had not ceased to complain that his poky little house was not suitable for a man in his position. It was the only one of brown brick in the dazzling white of the Crescent, and being at the Park Road end of it, she pointed out that it might easily be mistaken for a part of Park Road itself, which was a street composed of semi-detached brown brick villas inhabited by a very different class of people.

Only the recollection that it had been her extravagance as well as her husband's that had brought her and her family to their present impecunious condition made the General reply steadfastly to all these attacks that the house suited him very well and he did not intend to move from it.

He would have liked to see his elder niece enjoy herself more and he was as glad as she was when the period of mourning was over and Mrs Floyd was free to mix in what society Milchester could provide. It was difficult for the General's sister to enjoy herself unless she could find something to criticize in her friends' houses, servants, looks and dresses, comparing them with her own. But Cecily, he felt, was a different matter. Her good nature and willingness to listen made her welcome wherever she went, but young people were not encouraged by her mother to come to the house.

When she arrived home that morning Cecily found Mrs Floyd in her bedroom with a multitude of dresses spread out on her bed, trying to select one for Mrs Blades' dinner party.

"Now that I am out of that dreadful mourning, dearest, I can wear what I please," she told her daughter. For the prescribed period after her husband's death she had worn the hated widow's weeds, which gave place in time to greys and black and white, but now, Cecily observed, these too were to be replaced by colours.

"The question is, which shall I wear?" went on Mrs Floyd, studying the riot of purples, greens, pinks, reds and yellows on her bed. "If only I knew who would be there and what they will be wearing!"

"Well, we know that in all probability Mrs Blades will wear her brown silk," said Cecily soothingly.

"And those ugly cameos," agreed her mother. "She has the worst taste I have encountered, and as for those plain girls of hers, they always remind me of Worth's remark that young Englishwomen look like stable-boys dressed in tailor-mades."

"And then Mrs Kirby will be there I expect."

"And *she* will wear her purple velvet and amethysts."

"And Mrs Lavender—I know they are going."

"There is no knowing what Mrs Lavender will wear. She still loves the French brocades that were all the rage last winter. I shall never forget her at the Palace ball, in royal blue with silver stripes. Short fat women should *never* wear stripes. I wish I had the means to buy a length of French brocade, all the same. Mrs William Pitborough had such a beautiful pale green with white convolvulus woven into it. Everyone said it was the prettiest dress in the room." She sighed, studying the dresses on the bed with increasing dissatisfaction.

"And then Lady Scrimgour will be there, in her black velvet and diamonds," went on Cecily cheerfully. It was an unlucky remark.

"Her diamonds are nothing to what mine were," said Mrs Floyd bitterly. "I shall never forgive your uncle—kind as he has been to you all—for selling that beautiful set that your papa gave to me before he died."

"But, dearest, they had not been paid for and Uncle had to send them back to the jewellers."

"But he sold the furniture. That would have paid for them."

"Mamma, we have been over this so many times. You know that he had to sell the furniture to pay dear Papa's debts."

"He needn't have sold my dear little brougham and Dandy—such a sweet little horse and never any trouble in traffic. And that reminds me, I wonder if he remembered to order the cab for tonight?"

"I asked Pringle when I came in, and he said it had been ordered from Storey's and that Mr Storey is going to drive us himself. You always like Mr Storey to drive you."

"He certainly knows how to wait on one," agreed Mrs Floyd, still regretting her brougham. "But the cab will smell of the stables as it always does. I shall never believe that there was any need to sell my brougham and Dandy—any more than there was the need to rob me of my jewels."

It was useless to remind her that the livery stables where Dandy and the brougham were housed in London had not been paid for for over two years. Cecily turned cheerfully to the dresses on the bed and began to make suggestions as to which one was to be worn. "Nobody has seen these dresses," she reminded her mother. "And once the improvers are taken out and the material at the back gathered or pleated as Miss Kemp does so well, they will look quite new, won't they?"

"Yes, they must be altered. Bustles are as extinct as the Dodo this year." Mrs Floyd's eyes brightened, however, as Cecily held the different dresses against her, one at a time. "The rose pink is my favourite," she said at length. "The blue satin is a trifle too *decolleté* for a dinner party. I wish you were not so tall, then you could wear it, but blue is not your colour, is it? It makes you look sallow, dear, and your collar-bones are too pronounced for a dress as low-cut as this."

"What about the grey satin?" said Cecily, ignoring her complexion and her collar-bones.

"Oh no. I am tired of sad colours," said her mother, and they finally decided on the pink. When the dressmaker arrived that afternoon she happened to see Cecily in the hall, and she asked her what she was going to wear that evening.

"The white dress you altered for me for the Palace ball," Cecily said smiling. "I have no other."

Miss Kemp ran her eyes over the girl's slender figure thoughtfully. "I would dearly like to make you some new dresses, Miss Floyd," she said.

"Well, perhaps you will someday," Cecily said, and went to her room to take the white dress from her cupboard and regard its limp flounces with a rueful eye. But as it was unlikely that Mr Pitborough would be there that evening, she thought she would pass without any further accusations of being dowdy.

3

It was disconcerting to find that Mr Pitborough and his aunt were among Mrs Blades' guests, but as Cecily was separated from him by nearly the whole length of the table she saw little of him, although once or twice during the ten-course dinner she glanced across the large épergne that decorated the centre of the table to find his cool eyes studying her in a critical way that made her think he might still be finding fault with her poor little dress.

It made her double her efforts at searching for subjects of conversation with her partner, a young unmarried curate, whose attention was only too obviously given to Rosalind sitting opposite, and who, in consequence, met her well-meant efforts with monosyllables.

After dinner, while they were waiting for the gentlemen to join them, Cecily settled down to her usual

occupation at such gatherings, content to keep in the
background and listen to the conversation of others.
She was much amused by a discussion that developed
between old Lady Scrimgour and Mrs Blades on the
merits of a university education for young women.

"Cambridge University has, I believe, refused to
grant women degrees," Lady Scrimgour said at last,
knowing that she had met her match in the Colonel's
wife.

"And that is why, dear Lady Scrim, my eldest
daughter, in common with the rest of her year at
Newnham, is reading for honours. It is their ambition
to pass so high in the lists that from very shame the
university will be forced to grant them degrees."

"That's as may be." Unwilling as she was to give
way to bad manners in prolonging a discussion that
threatened to develop into an argument with her
hostess, Lady Scrimgour could not help remarking
that she did not see how university degrees could
possibly benefit the young women concerned. "They
may be men's equals in brains," she said, "I would
never dispute that, but physically they will always lag
a long way behind. I believe they have achieved some
success in the medical world, but I do not think many
woman doctors are to be found practising medicine.
I see no future for women graduates in arts beyond
that of superior governesses in modern girls' boarding schools, such as Cheltenham Ladies' College, under such estimable ladies as Miss Beale and Miss
Buss. My advice to the young women of today, Mrs
Blades, is to marry to enjoy the security of a home, to
bring up children to be a credit to themselves and their

husbands, and to leave matters outside that sphere
to men."

Mrs Blades good-naturedly conceded victory to
Lady Scrimgour and turning to Mrs Lavender asked
her how their preparations for their trip abroad were
progressing.

Mrs Lavender, looking almost as wide as she was
long in the royal blue striped dress that Mrs Floyd
so much deplored, at once asked for her sympathy.
Her husband had received a letter by the afternoon
post to tell him that the niece who was to have accompanied them had developed a bad throat and the doctor could not hold out any hope that she would be
well enough to come.

"What a pity," said Mrs Blades. "Nothing like
travel for a young gel." Her eyes dwelt for a moment
on Rosalind, who was chattering happily with some
of her young friends in a way that the Colonel's wife
dismissed as feather-brained. "Is there not another
niece who would be able to take her place in your
party?"

"She was the only one who could be spared," Mrs
Lavender said sadly.

"A friend, then," suggested kindly Mrs Blades,
her eyes resting significantly on Cecily, who had
moved nearer to her friend and was listening to Rosalind's absurdities with an indulgent smile. "Somebody
young—and yet sensible—who would be a companion
to your daughter?"

The advice and the look were not lost on Mrs
Lavender and she thought it over during the rest of
the evening.

The gentlemen returned and to Cecily's disgust and

astonishment Mr Pitborough, not content with having studied her throughout dinner as if she were some new and rare kind of animal seldom seen outside a zoo, now came and sat down beside her and thanked her gravely for having helped Janie to dress after the dancing class in the previous week. "Her nurse told me that she was being naughty," he said frowning. " 'Contrary' was the word she used."

"She was neither naughty nor contrary," said Cecily shortly, annoyed with the old woman. "She was only afraid that if she was not ready when you arrived with the dog-cart you would not wait for her. Possibly it was encouraged by her nurse, who, I daresay, like all old women, threatens her charge to gain her obedience." And then as he did not reply, but stiffened, looking taken aback and annoyed by her presumption, she added swiftly, "I beg your pardon, Mr Pitborough. I had no right to say that, but I can remember when I was little Janie's age my old nurse used to say she would give me to the coalman if I did not do as she wished. For years afterwards I was extremely frightened of coalmen." She hoped this would end the matter, but it did not. He remained seated beside her, gravely silent and frowning a little, and then he said almost as if he were trying to explain the position to himself as well as to her, "But I had promised I would be there with the dog-cart that afternoon, and I do not break my promises. At least"—for a moment he hesitated—'I have been forced to on one or two occasions when some important appointment at the bank has prevented me from leaving."

But surely nothing should have been more important than disappointing Janie? She thought again of the child with compassion, knowing from her own childhood how difficult it was for a child to match its hurrying steps to the slow ones of an old woman. "Now don't run, dear. My legs won't keep up with you!" The admonition came back to her over the years, reducing the speed of young legs that could not run fast enough to that of old legs that could not run at all.

She would have liked to suggest that he engage a younger nurse for Janie, but she did not want to invite a snub, and it was none of her business. So she sat silent and almost as if he read her thoughts he went on:

"Two years ago, acting on my mother's advice when she was visiting Oatesby, I engaged a younger woman for Janie. My mother interviewed the girl before going back to America, and told me that she had found a jewel. After she had gone, however, we discovered, my aunt and I, that the jewel was terrifying the child with stories of ghosts and hobgoblins who would come after her if she dared to stir from her bed. The woman was making assignments with one of the grooms and did not wish to be tied to a nursery at night. So I dismissed her and had Nurse Appleby back again. She is old but very devoted, and her threats are not serious enough to do a great deal of harm."

Cecily bent her head but did not reply, having no wish to enter into a prolonged discussion of Mr Pitborough's domestic affairs, and she was relieved when music was suggested and Mrs Blades asked her to sing.

Although her voice had not had the training of some of the others present, it was a charming one and

much in request at evening parties. But the thought
of standing up in her shabby dress in front of the
assembled company, and Mr Pitborough in particular, daunted her, and she excused herself by saying
she was a trifle hoarse—and indeed her perseverance
in entertaining the curate at dinner fully justified such
an excuse. She volunteered, however, to accompany
the songs of others, thankful to escape to the piano,
but even with her fingers occupied with the keys she
found that she was still teased by Charles Pitborough,
who continued to watch her with that cool, calculating
air of his until she began to wonder if he was thinking
of engaging her perhaps as a governess in his household. His conversation, coupled with his almost re-
lentless scrutiny, put the idea into her head, to be
dismissed at once as absurd. Mr Charles Pitborough
surely knew that General Masterson's niece was not
likely to go out as a governess, even to such an exalted
place as Oatesby. She was relieved, all the same, when
he was asked to make up a four at whist in the Colonel's study and she did not see him again for the rest
of the evening.

Mrs Lavender was still thinking about their spoiled
tour as she lighted her candle and went upstairs
to bed that night, and after her maid had gone and
her husband had left his dressing-room she told him
that she wished they could find somebody to accompany them in place of poor Laura. "It will be so dull
for Rosalind with only two old fogies like us for her
companions," she said, and refrained from adding
that she was afraid there might be undesirable young
men among their fellow tourists from whom their
daughter would be protected by a steady young

woman friend. "Do you think, by dear, that Miss Floyd would like to come with us?"

"Miss Floyd?" Mr Lavender thought it over while he adjusted his nightcap, and at length he said that he did not see why not. "The tickets are paid for and the rooms booked for four people. It seems a pity to waste a ticket and to reduce our party."

"And Mr Ferndean only joins us for a week at Lucerne," went on Mrs Lavender placidly, "so there would be no danger there."

"Oh, my dear, do not let your mind run so much on love and matrimony!" said her husband good-humouredly. "You know as well as I do that Giles Ferndean has no eyes for anyone but Rosalind. I think Miss Floyd might have a very steadying influence on her, while at the same time providing the young society you think she may need. The expense of it will of course be my affair. Miss Floyd will come as our guest."

"There will be new clothes for her to find," said Mrs Lavender anxiously. "I would not like to put the dear old General to extra expense."

"Her clothes can be our business as well." Mr Lavender brushed it aside. "What gewgaws she will need will not be many—a few dresses or so."

"It will be a pleasure to see the poor girl dressed in something better than her mother's cast-offs," agreed Mrs Lavender as she climbed into her side of the large double bed. "Will you go and see the General and Mrs Floyd tomorrow, dear? There is not much time if we are to leave at the end of April."

"I will see the General and obtain his consent before I interview Miss Floyd's mother. I think we shall find that he will be as pleased as she is the contrary." Mr Lavender saw that the windows were closed against the treacherous March night air before he too got into bed.

Mr Lavender was right. Mrs Floyd alone was annoyed by his invitation to her daughter to join his party: the rest of the family were frankly envious, the General delighted.

"The Lavenders are very well-to-do," complained Mrs Floyd to her brother that evening after the younger ones were in bed while Cecily was busy cutting out some new shirts for her two brothers at the dining-room table. "It would not have hurt them to include me in their party. I will not say that I am attracted to the idea of a Cook's tour, but they know what a miserable time I have had over the past few years, and it would have been the very thing to take my mind off my troubles. You would have thought that anybody with any feeling would have thought of it at once."

"My dear Louisa!" The General regarded his sister impatiently: she was seated comfortably in an armchair with her small feet resting on a footstool as she indulged in her usual pastime of playing with her rings and bracelets. "Can you not be less selfish? Surely you do not grudge Cecily a holiday abroad in the company of friends?"

If anyone else had spoken to her like that Mrs Floyd would have indulged in a fit of hysterics, but she knew her brother would have none of it. She said in an injured voice: "I am as devoted to Cecily as I am to all my children, and it is on her behalf that I do not like the thought of her going on this trip. I know perfectly well why the Lavenders are anxious to take her: simply so that she can be there to keep an eye on that flighty little Rosalind. That is all they are doing it for, and, of course, having paid for it, they will expect her to give services for her keep."

"There you are wrong," said the General. "I told Mr Lavender this morning that I shall be delighted for Cecily to accompany them, but that of course her railway tickets and hotel bills and other expenses will be entirely my affair. She will need some new clothes too, but I have talked to her about that and she seems to think that your little dressmaker will be able to make all that she needs."

"There is no need to spend anything on her clothes," said Louisa Floyd peevishly. "I have plenty of dresses that can be altered for her."

"No. She is having none of your cast-offs for this holiday: she deserves better than that," said her brother firmly. "After Reginald's debts were paid there was sufficient money left to invest so that you had a small income of your own. I had hoped that you would find it enough not only to clothe yourself, but with a little care to clothe Cecily as well as the boys and Bella. But sometimes I have been forced to believe that except for an occasional party dress for Bella, and suits for the boys when their old ones were no longer fit to wear, everything has gone on yourself."

"My dearest Reginald never grudged me anything," whimpered Mrs Floyd. "He always told me to order what I wanted and not to consider the cost."

"And that was why he did not leave a penny when he died," said the General rather brutally.

"How can you be so cruel?" His sister's blue eyes filled and he relented, laying his hand on her shoulder.

"Come, my dear, I did not mean to be unkind, but I am determined that Cecily shall have her holiday and that she shall enjoy it as she should. She is a sensible girl and I know she will not involve her old uncle in unnecessary expense."

Mrs Floyd said she thought she would go up to bed. She went into the dining-room to take Cecily away from her cutting-out to come and help her out of her dress and curl her hair and said disagreeably that she supposed her poor brothers would have to wait for their shirts now until she had got back from her holiday in Europe. She would never have time to make them before she went.

"No," Cecily agreed cheerfully. "But I am going to do them up in a parcel tomorrow and take them to Mrs Chadwell. She does such beautiful hemming, and I am sure she will be kind enough to make them for me before I leave."

Nothing that her mother could say damped her pleasure in the thought of the holiday that lay in front of her, although at the same time she was a little dismayed at the expense that it had laid on her uncle, a fact that was to be dwelt upon by Mrs Floyd at every opportunity during the next four weeks.

On consulting Mrs Lavender the next day, however, Cecily found that the travellers had been advised to take as few clothes as they could, because of the problem of travelling with heavy luggage, which was not advised.

A serge coat over a warm dress for traveling in colder climates, and an alpaca one to cover thin dresses in Italy were essential, and she would need a pair of stout boots for climbing the mountains in Switzerland. "They need not be studded," Mrs Lavender added. "Mr Lavender was told it would be better if we leave that to the Swiss boot-makers to do for us when we get there." When they left Paris they were to go by way of Fontainebleau and Dijon to Geneva and then on to Lausanne, Friberg, and Interlaken to Lucerne.

"Shall I take an evening dress?" asked Cecily.

"One good silk dress suitable for theatre going I think, and two or three light dresses for wearing in Italy where I believe it is very warm in June." Mrs Lavender took the girl's hand and kissed her. "I am very glad you are coming with us, my dear. It will be a great pleasure to have you."

Cecily thanked her again and went on to see Miss Kemp, and they had a delightful afternoon laying out the money that the General had given her for her clothes in materials and styles and trimmings.

"As for your evening dress," Miss Kemp said, "I have a length of beautiful gold silk by me: it was given me by a lady after her daughter died. The young lady was to have a ball-dress made of it but her mother could not bear to have it back and told me to keep it for linings or anything I wanted. It is much too good for that however, and as it has lain for some years now it may have worn a little in the folds, which is why I could never charge you for it. Miss Floyd. I will have it out and see what I can make of it for you." The material was brought out of its paper wrapping and declared by the little dressmaker to be just Miss Floyd's colour, and although Cecily could see no wear in the folds she insisted that she would only charge her for the making.

The next day Cecily took the bundle of shirts to Mrs Chadwell and found the old lady in the garden, hanging out a quantity of washing. When she told her what she wanted Mrs Chadwell, her utterance somewhat impeded by a clothes peg in her mouth, said that she would have a look at the shirts, and if it was only plain sewing that was wanted she thought she could manage it.

Cecily waited while she finished hanging out her washing, and looking at the number of towels and sheets and pillow cases on the line thought that Mr Tilverton must be very particular about his clean linen. Here she was mistaken: however much Mr Tilverton might be slighted by his uncle Mrs Chadwell knew what was due to one of her babies.

She took Cecily into her small front parlour, and having examined the shirts and the work that was required said that she would do them with pleasure, as she would have more time now that Mr Tilverton had gone back to London.

"I did not know that he had gone." Cecily wondered that Rosalind had not told her.

"He went yesterday. Mind you, I don't know for sure how he is to manage with that bad arm of his. He finds it mortal hard to use it yet, and it's a good thing as 'twastn't his right arm as it's all writing what he has to do in that there office or whatever they calls it. It do seem hard that his lordship should treat his own flesh and blood like that, but he always was a hard man. Not that I'd put up with it if I was Mr Barnaby. 'Why don't you go to his lordship,' I said, 'and tell him to his face you've not got enough money to live on?' 'I wouldn't go, not if I was dying, Chaddy,' he says. 'My uncle's done all I ever want him to do for me.' Never was one to put hisself forwards, wasn't Mr Barnaby. Not like his lordship's children, all go from the moment they was born. Directly the midwife went her ladyship would put her new baby into my arms. 'He's yours now, Chaddy,' she would say, like as if she was thankful to be rid of him. All boys they was, one after another. But they wasn't like Mr Barnaby, Mr Rupert's child. Delicate from the start, he clung to me as his cousins never did, poor little fellow."

"So he has gone back to London?" Cecily said watching the billowing sheets on the line.

"Yes." The old woman hesitated for a moment and then she said, "As you are going for this holiday with Mr and Mrs Lavender, you will be a friend of Miss Lavender's. I'm thinkin'?"

"I am her friend," said Cecily smiling.

"Then perhaps you would not mind giving her a letter what Mr Barnaby left behind. I don't know as he ought to have writ to her, mind, and I don't know as I ought to give it to you for her, like this, but I've seen them in the lane time after time, when she took her little dog for walks, and if ever I see a young couple in love—and so suited to each other—it's them."

Cecily looked down at the wrinkled old face that was so full of tenderness for her baby, Barnaby, and she thought she would try to pull the moon from the sky if he wanted it. And Rosalind Lavender was indeed akin to that moon had she but known it. Yet she held out her hand for the letter.

"I will give it to her," she said gently. "I know she will be pleased to have it."

* * * * *

Although Mrs Floyd dropped the broadest of hints to Mrs Lavender whenever the two ladies met it did not seem to occur to her or to her husband to include Cecily's mother in their invitation, and it remained steadfastly for Cecily alone. She was forced to reserve her complaints for when she was alone with her daughter.

As time went on and the day of the departure approached they became manifold. She did not know how she was going to manage with Cecily enjoying herself abroad with those Lavenders, leaving her mother to work herself to the bone. Who would take Bella to her music lessons and her dancing classes and fetch her again in the afternoons? Their uncle had no servants to spare for such errands. And who was gonig to mend the boys' clothes and see that they got off to school in the mornings? And who was going to do her hair?

"You know I have not had a lady's maid since your poor papa died," she said. "It is only because I have taught you not to be clumsy that I have been able to save the expense of one."

Then she went back to the boys, who attended the Cathedral School in the Close. It was quite a walk from the Crescent, and Cecily knew quite well that her mother was unable to rise from her bed until after ten in the mornings, and that her breakfast was always brought up to her room. With Cecily not there to prepare it for her she was going to endure black looks from the General's housekeeper, Mrs Barrington, and the tray would be set out anyhow, not daintily as she liked to see it, nor the toast as she liked it either.

"I shall never forget that week last winter when you had a bad cold and the doctor insisted that it was that Russian influenza that everyone was having, and that you should stay in bed, which in my opinion was quite unnecessary. Nobody stays in bed for bad colds unless they have a fever. I have never had so many wretched breakfasts in my life. Everything cold and the toast burnt." It was quite extraordinary, she added, how the selfishness of one person could throw out an entire household.

The last week came: they were to leave Milchester on the Friday afternoon to be ready for an early start from London on the following day, and by the time Thursday came Cecily was on the point of calling on the Lavenders to tell them that she would have to cancel the trip.

And, indeed if it had not been for Charles Pitborough that is exactly what she would have done.

4

The shirts were sent home on Thursday morning, beautifully done, and Cecily escaped from the rising crescendo of her mother's lamentations and went to Love Lane early that afternoon to settle her account with Mrs Chadwell before fetching Bella from her dancing class for the last time.

It was a beautiful day, the sky an April blue with small woolly clouds puffing across it, and as she reached a seat in one of the winding paths in the park with time in hand before she need make her appearance at the Assembly Rooms, she sat down to think about her holiday and to reason things out. She was not at all sure by this time that the trip abroad that had seemed so splendid, so unexpected and delightful a month ago, had not as her mother said, been seized upon by herself as a selfish way of escaping from her responsibilities.

She had been there a few minutes in frowning contemplation of the park and the trees, where the buds of chestnut and lime and bursts of elder and hawthorn leaves were beginning to show signs of spring, when she heard her name and she turned her head quickly to see Charles Pitborough with a large dog whom he appeared to be exercising.

She returned his greeting coolly and expected him to walk on when he called the dog to heel and sat down beside her.

"The very person I wanted to see," he said. "I would like to speak to you, Miss Floyd, if you can spare me a few moments."

"Of course." The thought that he might indeed be considering her seriously as a governess for Janie came back rather forcibly to her mind.

For a moment he did not seem to know how to proceed: he sat there beside her frowning and digging with the point of his malacca at the mossy path, and then he said abruptly, looking ahead of him at the cathedral spire rising above the grey old roofs of the town beyond the trees, "My aunt is leaving me at the end of the summer. When my wife died Aunt Hannah let her house in Gloucestershire to come and look after Janie and myself. Her tenants are leaving at Michaelmas however, and she wishes to go back there to live, taking her parrot with her." A ghost of a smile touched his lips. "I shall not be sorry for that and neither will Janie. The wretched bird terrifies her, and the only time she tried to make friends with it, it nearly bit her finger to the bone. Before she goes however, my aunt wants me to find somebody to take her place." He paused, the frown deepening on his face, and she dismissed the idea of the governess and wondered if he were going to suggest that she should become his housekeeper. It seemed improbable, and yet, remembering the cool way in which he had studied her lately whenever they chanced to meet, it was possible, and while she remained silent, half amused and half indignant, he went on:

"For Janie's sake the lady would of course have to be younger than my aunt, but at the same time responsible enough to run my household, and my aunt suggests that I should—in short—marry again." The poking stick into the moss became more vicious now as without looking at her he asked flatly: "Would such a position appeal to you, Miss Floyd?"

The way the question was put as well as the completely cool explanation that had proceeded it, took her breath away. So this was what her well-meant interference over Janie had brought her to, and all amusement gone, she got to her feet. "As I do not think you can be serious," she said crisply, "I will not trouble to answer you. I have no time to waste on hypothetical questions of that sort, and it is time I started for the Assembly Rooms and my sister's dancing class."

His reply was unexpected. He gripped her arm and pulled her down again on the seat beside him. "Sit down and don't be a fool," he said brusquely. "If I had not been serious I would not have troubled you. It is a purely business arrangement that I would like you to consider: if I had a young woman in my house without my aunt there to chaperone her, before the first week was out the town would be saying that she was my mistress, and that is a risk that I will not take,

for Janie's sake. I have been studying you ever since
my aunt told me of her decision: you seemed to me to
be a sensible woman and not too young. I suppose
you are twenty-eight or maybe older?"

"I am not yet twenty-two," she said quickly.

"I did not think you were so young." He was obviously put out. "You look considerably older."

"That is because I am dowdy," she said, and saw
him glance at her for the first time. "That is the de-
scription you gave to Mrs Blades I believe at the
Palace ball?"

"Did I?" There was surprise now in that keen
glance. "If I did Mrs Blades had no right to repeat it
to you."

"She did not. My mother overheard you and told
me later that night."

"Then I do not apologize. Had I wanted her to hear
it, it would have been unpardonable, but as such a
contingency did not occur to me I was scarcely to
blame. It was that very—dowdiness—of yours that
made me think you might have more sense than the
empty-headed girls that seem to abound in and around
Milchester." His eyes rested on her shabby blue serge
dress and jacket without interest. "As I said before,
what I am suggesting to you, Miss Floyd, is purely a
business arrangement. If you will go through a marriage ceremony with me to quieten the gossips that is
all that will be required of you. You would have your
own rooms at Oatesby and I promise you that I should
not intrude upon you in any way. My interest in
women is a very limited one." Again he paused, and
then as she did not reply, he said impatiently, "Well?
What have you to say to it? You are at liberty if you

wish to have time in which to think it over. But I am a rich man. You could have what money you liked—within reason."

The qualification almost made her smile. Then quite suddenly she thought she knew how to deal with him. She said sweetly: "Thank you, Mr Pitborough, but I do not require any time in which to think about your offer. I will give you my answer here and now. I am quite prepared to marry you on your conditions, if on your side you are prepared to marry me on mine."

She was gratified to observe that she had surprised him even more than he had surprised her.

"And what might your conditions be?" he asked with more than a touch of irony.

"That my family comes with me to Oatesby," she said firmly.

"Your family?" He did not understand her.

"My mother, my sister and my two brothers," she explained.

He did not take a moment in which to consider it. "That is quite impossible."

"So it seems that there is no more to be said between us." Once more she got up and this time he did not attempt to detain her. "I suppose I should thank you for doing me the honour of asking me to be your wife," she said. "But under the circumstances I am not quite sure that it was an honour, nor that my thanks are necessary."

She walked away down the path leaving him staring after her and still poking at the path with his stick. After the Palace ball his cousin's wife had asked him if he did not think Miss Floyd had very pretty eyes and he had replied that he had not noticed

them, but latterly he had observed that Cecily's eyes
were large and hazel and had remarkably fine lashes.
They could however register extreme anger, as they
had done just now, and he thought back over what
he had said to her ruefully, knowing that he had been
unforgivably off-hand, if not downright rude. He had
in fact, in trying to put his case to her, only suc-
ceeded in addressing her as if she were a board meeting, and no woman, however dowdy she might be,
would appreciate that. The trouble with women, he
thought with exasperation, was that they were too
damned emotional. And he had finished with all emotion on the day that his lovely heartless Gussie died,
leaving him sucked dry.

He got up and calling the retriever, walked back
slowly to the bank.

* * * * *

Cecily said nothing of Charles Pitborough's proposal to her family, hoping that he would forget the
whole thing as she intended to forget it, but here she
underrated the determination of the man.

The following morning she was in her room putting
a few last items into the morocco leather dressing-
case that had been her uncle's present to her.

"Sorry the fittings are only nickel," he said gruffly
when she tried to thank him. "Would have liked them
to be silver or ivory—but beyond my means. It will be
as useful though, no doubt." In it there was the small
morocco leather purse that her brothers and sister
had given her and they too had apologized because
it was not larger. "It cost three shillings and sixpence,"
the elder boy, Leonard, had told her. "And a penny

a week pocket money takes an awful lot of saving, Cis, specially when Bella will spend hers on ha'penny bull's eyes. We had to borrow several weeks ahead from Uncle Hump."

Dear Uncle Hump. Cecily's eyes misted a little as she made sure she had everything. She was dressed ready for her journey in her new brown serge travelling dress and the jacket that was to go over it lay on the bed with her gloves and hat. The passport that the General had travelled to London to obtain for her was in the dressing-case with her brushes and overnight necessities, because although passports were not necessary in Switzerland or Italy her uncle told her they could be useful in an emergency, if one had to go to the British Consul for help, or in the event of fetching letters from a foreign post office.

The domed trunk made of cane covered with black American cloth was strapped and ready to be taken downstairs by Pringle directly the Lavenders' carriage came to the door that afternoon, and she was looking about her to see that nothing had been forgotten when there was a knock at the door and Mrs Barrington came in.

"The master would like a word with you in the smoking-room, if you can spare the time, miss," the housekeeper said. She looked from the trunk to Cecily's new dress with undisguised approval. "And may I say, miss, how glad we all are in the hall that you are going on this holiday? We hope that you will enjoy every moment of it, and we would like you to take this with you as a small memento from us all." She put a packet into the girl's hand and when she opened it Cecily found six white lawn handkerchiefs, each embroidered with her initials in one corner.

"We each did two," said Mrs Barrington. "Except Nellie. Being as she's kitchen-maid her hands are too rough to do fine work, but she was so eager to do something that we let her hem them—which is why the hems aren't as even as I should like. The initials too are not as well done as we should have liked by reason of there being so little time."

Cecily thanked her warmly, her eyes smarting again as she said she would put them into her dressing-case at once. And then she went down to her uncle.

"My dear," he said, coming forward to take her hand. "I have had a strange letter from Mr Charles Pitborough this morning."

"Oh no!" The smile left her face and she gave a small gasp of dismay. "What does he say?"

"I see that you know what it is about," he said smiling. "Sit down, my dear. He says that yesterday afternoon he asked you to be his wife, and that you —made conditions that he found it then impossible to meet. On thinking it over, however, he fancies a solution might be found between you that would be agreeable to both parties, and he would like to come and see you about it tomorrow morning. He does not know, apparently, that you leave Milchester this afternoon."

"There is no reason why he should know." Cecily took a little time to reply. "What a tiresome man he is to be sure. It is true that he did ask me to marry him, Uncle Hump. But as he seemed to look on it as a business contract and not as a human relationship at all, I made certain conditions on my side, which, as he says in that letter, he did not feel inclined to meet.

And there I hoped the matter would end."

"*You* made conditions?" Her uncle spoke gravely, but his eyes were twinkling. "May I ask what they were, my love?"

"I said that if I were to marry him I would have to bring my family with me, and he said that it would be impossible. I daresay he thought that on the day they moved into Oatesby he would move out, and I do not blame him for that, much as I dislike him." She saw her uncle's face and laughed. "Uncle Hump, all he wanted was a sort of glorified housekeeper—that is to say a lady younger than his aunt to be Janie's mamma and his own hostess. He explained his reasons most carefully. He could not invite me to live in his house with propriety unless we went through a form of marriage. I assure you he did not consider me at all, except in thinking that my dowdy clothes and grave manner would suit the position he was offering me admirably. There was no word of affection spoken between us and never will be."

"He sounds a cold fish." The General chuckled. "You have more courage than I have all the same. I should have thought he was a daunting chap to thwart. I doubt if you will have heard the last of him, but in the meantime what am I to tell him, Cecily?"

"Tell him that I am leaving today for the Continent with Mr and Mrs Lavender, and that if he should be of the same mind when I return at the end of June I will discuss it with him again." Cecily spoke calmly and sensibly, and once again he chuckled.

"I will do as you say," he said. "But if there *had* been any affection between you I warn you that I would not have let you off so lightly. You would have had to see the man before you left this afternoon to tell him that your only reason for wanting him to take your family into his house was to relieve your old uncle of what you consider to be a burden to him. Yes, Cecily my love, I can see through this 'condition' of yours quite easily, but as you say there is no question of it being anything more than a business interprize I think you are wise not to consider him. In marriage I am pretty sure that the only consideration that should enter a woman's mind is whether she loves the man who wants to marry her. You will think me a romantic old fool, I daresay, because I have never married. Well, the girl I was in love with many years ago married somebody else, and I never found anyone I would have liked to put in her place. But that is past history—long past."

He broke off, his mind for a moment occupied with the past and then he added: "I will not say anything of this to your mamma, my dear. If I did, I doubt if life would be supportable for any of us for a time."

"I know." If Mrs Floyd were to know that her plain, dowdy daughter had had the temerity to refuse the proposal of one of the richest men in the district, she would probably take to her bed permanently, and in any case there would be such a scene that Cecily would not be able to start on her journey that afternoon. "It will be our secret, Uncle Hump, and I am quite sure that Mr Pitborough will keep it to himself too."

The General went to a drawer in his desk and took from it a crisp Bank of England five-pound note. "Keep that with your passport, my love," he said. "If there should be any difficulty, or if any emergency should arise when you are out of England, then an English five-pound bank note is currency everywhere."

"Darling Uncle Hump!" She kissed him warmly. "I do hope Mamma will not be tiresome after I am gone."

"Don't give it a thought." He patted her shoulder. "And don't forget that I survived the Crimea War!"

Fortunately the complaints of the past weeks had developed into an injured silence where Mrs Floyd was concerned, and she only broke it that morning to say that she would not be coming down to lunch as she could not eat a mouthful. Whereupon the General went up to his sister's room and told her in no uncertain terms to mend her conduct.

"You have got to get over your sulks and come down and behave kindly to Cecily before she leaves," he told her sternly. "She will be gone in an hour or so and you will not be seeing her for a couple of months."

"She is a naughty, selfish girl, and she has shown herself to be quite heartless, over this ridiculous trip of hers." Mrs Floyd's anger turned to petulance. "I know it is no good saying anything to you Humphrey. You have encouraged her all along. It is all the doing of those wretched Lavenders. I wish they had not come to live here. If they had not filled her head with such notions she would not have dreamed of going off in this fashion."

She came down to luncheon declaring to the last that she did not know how they were going to manage for the next three months, and after the Lavenders' carriage arrived to fetch Cecily and her luggage that afternoon, moving off down the Crescent with its load of smiling faces and waving handkerchiefs, bound for the railway station, she said to Bella with a sigh. "Who will fetch you from your dancing classes and your music lessons now, my poor darling, I really do not know."

Whereupon the General, his temper worn thin, turned on her and remarked with asperity that it would not hurt her to fetch her daughter herself.

"But if it comes to that I'll have to take the gig out to fetch her," he said. "Hey, Bella? You'll enjoy that, won't you?"

Bella declared she would love it and danced round him until Mrs Floyd said she made her head ache. In the end however she decided not to make a scene: Bella was not like Cecily. She did not know where her smelling salts were and she would be forced to fetch them herself.

So she sighed again and said she supposed they would manage somehow and the General said he was sure they would manage very well, and he went down to the Liberal Club for the rest of the day.

5

Charles Pitborough felt extremely put out when he received the General's letter. At first he was inclined to tear it up and dismiss all further thought of Miss Floyd from his mind, and then he thought better of it. At dinner that night he asked his aunt if she knew where the Lavenders were going.

"On this Cook's tour of theirs, do you mean?" she asked.

"I did not know it was to be a Cook's tour," he said. "In fact I know nothing about it."

"Neither do I," she said. "And I have not been sufficiently interested to find out. I only know that they are to be away until the end of June and that they have taken Miss Floyd with them, in place of a niece who was unable to go. Why do you ask?"

"Oh, simply a matter of business," he replied quickly and changed the subject by criticizing the leg of mutton. "I do not think this has hung long enough," he complained. "It is as tough as whip-leather."

It was unlike him to complain of his food and she wondered what was worrying him and put it down as something to do with the bank. She said she would speak to Mrs Bolingbroke about the mutton. "I don't suppose it will make any difference though. She tells me that Rampart thinks he can send almost anything to Oatesby nowadays. The orders are not large enough for him. You should do more entertaining, my dear."

"I am afraid I cannot alter my ways to suit my butcher, and I daresay there are others in Milchester who will be more obliging."

"I think you should entertain more than you do all the same, Charles. You are a young man still—not yet forty. It is not good for you to sit here alone with an old woman for company night after night, brooding over bank business. You need younger people about you."

"I beg your pardon but I do not agree with you. I do not need younger people about me—except Pudding." That night however, after his aunt had retired and the abominable parrot had been covered for the night, he opened the piano in the drawing-room where they had been sitting and played for a time, trying to forget about the situation in which he found himself with regard to one young person in particular. His aunt, hearing him, wondered again what was wrong. In the old days he was a very fine pianist and when Gussie was alive he had played accompaniments for her songs night after night, but it was seldom that he touched the piano these days.

The fact was that Charles was still very angry with

Cecily for having treated him with such scant respect. He thought it quite extraordinary that General Masterson's penniless niece could have had the impudence, as well as the imprudence, to reject him so summarily. She knew quite well that no man in his senses would have that empty-headed mother of hers living in the same house with him, while her schoolboy brothers and her tom-boy sister would turn the place into a bear-garden. His poor little Pudding would be completely overlooked in such a family: it was unreasonable of her to suggest it. He shut the piano and went into the library to write his weekly letter to his Uncle Joseph Orde, unwilling to admit that what had rankled most had been the calm way in which Cecily had sent a message by the General that she would discuss it with him again when she came home at the end of June, as if she were conferring an honour on him.

The butler brought his brandy and water and left it on its silver tray on the writing table and said good night. But although the brandy mellowed him a little it did nothing to lessen his sense of personal injury. He began to wonder if Miss Floyd had laid down the terms she had because she knew that he would not accept them and because she had no intention of accepting him either. If so this personal rejection was more hurtful still. Even if a woman had been treated as a board meeting she could surely exhibit a little more human feeling.

"I won't think about her any more," he said as he went upstairs to bed in the wee hours with his letter still unfinished. "She has pestered me enough." Which was surely unfair considering how little Cecily had said and done to encourage—let alone pester him—since he had known her.

The next day however he found that the thought of her came obstinately between him and the problems on his desk in his room at the bank: he kept thinking of her as he had seen her first at the Palace ball, in her shabby dress, her dark hair with its straight fringe and only the hint of a wave, parted severely down the middle and drawn back into a great knot on the nape of her neck. He kept thinking of her too as he had seen her last Thursday, equally shabby but with her head held high and her eyes as clearly honest as they had been at the ball. Contemptuous and defiant too, as if she did not care what he or anybody else might think of her. It was ridiculous to let his mind dwell on her so much when he had shown her how little he regarded her as a woman, but it was also extremely irritating when he had simply wanted to engage a young lady to run his household and be a Mamma for this little girl without raising a scandal about his ears, to find one ideally suited to his purpose and yet so utterly disinclined to consider it.

At the end of the day when old Summerscales came in with some letters for him to sign he asked him if Mr Lavender had left any address where business communications could be forwarded to him while he was out of England. "I understand he is to be away for two months," he added.

"Oh yes, sir. The first address he left with me was the Hotel Schweizerhof in Lucerne. He plans to be there a week I believe before he goes on to Italy."

"And in Italy?" asked Charles idly, tapping his

penholder on the table as if he had not much interest in the answer to his question.

"He is going first of all to Venice, to the Great Britain Hotel, which he told me is on the Grand Canal. Sounds very beautiful, sir, though I'm not very fond of the sea myself. He plans to be there a fortnight—or maybe three weeks—before he goes to Rome on his way home."

"And when does he think he will arrive in Venice?"

"End of May, sir."

"You have made a note of all this I take it?"

"Yes, sir."

Charles finished signing the letters and told the old man to be off home. "I'll bet the younger ones have cleared off long ago," he said.

"Well, sir, it's this lawn tennis," said old Summerscales mildly. "They come on a Saturday bringing their tennis flannels and their bats with them and the moment it's struck five they change and off they go to have what they call a "knock-up" before the light goes." He shook his head. "It wasn't like that in my young days, Mr Charles. There were no lawn tennis clubs for us. Many's the time I've sat here on a Saturday evening working till seven or eight when your father was alive."

"We must move with the times," Charles told him tolerantly. As the head clerk reached the door with the letters ready for the post he called him back for a moment. "Sir Matthew Billing," he said. "Have we had any more news of him since I received that eccentric communication from—where was it?"

"Madrid, sir."

"That's it. He complained bitterly that the Spanish

ladies were not as beautiful as he had been led to
expect." Charles exchanged a fleeting smile with the
old clerk. "One would have thought that at eighty it
would not have been a matter of great concern, but
Sir Matthew is Sir Matthew."

"We have heard no more of him, sir. He may be on
his way home."

"I daresay he is, full of some crack-pot scheme for
the bank to invest in, and he will be very angry when
I refuse, but that is Sir Matthew's way." Charles said
good night and told Summerscales that he would lock
up, and after he had gone the acting Senior Partner
stood at the window of Joseph Orde's room for a
while, watching through the wire screen the men from
the offices in the city and the women from the shops
that preferred to close on Saturday evening rather
than the more popular Wednesday afternoons, as they
hurried past the bank on their way home.

As he stood there with his hands in his pockets his
aunt's words came back to him: "You should entertain more—you are a young man—you need young
people about you." But he did not feel young any
more. He had not felt young since Gussie died and
he did not think he would ever feel young again.

He went back to his desk and found Sir Matthew
Billing's letter and studied it with amusement until
his carriage came for him, and then, rather than keep
the horses waiting, he went home.

Over dinner that night, after she had chided him for
being so late on a Saturday, his aunt asked him if
he found the meat more tender.

"Tender enough, thank you." He semed preoccu-
pied. "Do not worry about it, Aunt Hannah."

"But I do worry." Later on when the servants had left them to dessert and port wine she asked him if he had thought any more about the advice she had given him before Christmas.

"What advice, Aunt?"

"You know quite well," she said sharply. "I told you to look about for a wife, Charles. I shall be moving to Gloucestershire at Michaelmas and these things take time to arrange."

"I have no intention of hurrying into a second marriage, thank you," he said coldly. "My first was disastrous enough for any man."

"You cannot dwell on the past," she told him, rather more kindly however. "You would do much better to forget it—and Augusta. She treated you abominably and it was a mercy that she died."

For a moment he said nothing, his thoughts going back to his wife: so lovely to look at, so gay and witty, so terribly and heart-breakingly unfaithful. He said abruptly: "I have been very grateful for your help over these last years, you know that, my dear aunt. But I do not want to keep you away from your own home any longer, and you need not have the slightest concern for me when the time comes for you to leave Oatesby. Nurse Appleby manages Pudding very well: the child loves her and the old woman is very devoted. I do not think there is any real reason why I should marry again. I have an excellent housekeeper in Mrs Bolingbroke."

"I wish you would not call Janie by that ridiculous name," complained his aunt. "And she will not remain a child for ever. She will soon need more than the daily governess she has now. Miss Forrester may be a clergyman's daughter, but she is extremely old-fashioned in her teaching methods, which appear to me to be largely based on Mrs Edgeworth!"

"She is teaching her to read and write and that is all that Pudding needs at the moment," he replied, and his aunt said rather crossly that she would leave him to his port and she went back to the drawing-room and her embroidery and her parrot.

That night once more he spent a great deal of time thinking about Cecily Floyd, and it occurred to him that it might be a good thing if he were to see the young lady before she came home. It might show her that he was not prepared to put up with the whim of a twenty-two-year-old girl.

He could for example visit his sister Miriam, who was usually in Venice in June, and he would take Janie with him, as an excuse. It was time she met her Italian cousins.

This idea seemed a good one until he remembered the way his sister had of seeing through excuses, and not wishing to have any that might not seem reasonable, he thought it might be an excellent idea to take Barnaby Tilverton with him too, on account of the young man's health. The next morning at breakfast he horrified his aunt by announcing his intention of travelling to London that day.

"On a Sunday?" she said. "What would your dear father have said?"

"As he is no longer here to say it," he replied equably, "I cannot hazard a guess in that direction. I will trust you to take Pudding to church for me in my absence. I shall be back I hope this evening."

"But won't your business wait until tomorrow?" she asked.

"Not this particular line of business," he replied.

On arriving at Euston he took a cab to a quarter of London much given to cheap lodging houses, and in a dreary little street he told the cabby to wait while he knocked at the door of a house in a terrace that looked as if it had started going downhill when it was built and had never stopped. He asked the slatternly woman who answered his knock by shouting up from the basement to demand what he wanted, if Mr Tilverton was in.

"Nothing to stop you going up to see," she said, not shouting quite so loudly and looking from him to the cab with some curiosity. "Door's on the latch. It's the second floor back."

He pushed open the door and climbed the narrow stairs, wondering how his young friend could endure the oil-clothed passages and the awful smell of washing, stews and cabbage that came up through the house from the basement like some abominable form of incense. On arriving at the second floor back he knocked again on a door from which most of the paint had been knocked off, and a weary young voice told him to enter.

He went in and found Mr Tilverton there, sitting at a table under a narrow window, translating French into English in a round, legible hand.

"Mr Pitborough!" On seeing his visitor he got to his feet quickly, flushing. "I am sorry you have had to come here, but I am doing my best to defray my debt to the bank." He indicated the book and the sheets of manuscript on the table with a pallid smile.

"I have obtained work translating this book for a publisher in Water Lane—he is to pay me a pound for each book that I translate for him, and as you see, I am half-way through the first."

"My dear fellow, I did not come to dun you!" Charles was horrified that he should think him capable of such a thing. "Your debt—as you call it, though I would like to call it nothing of the sort—is for only ten pounds. What of it? Can you not do as I suggested before you left Milchester and let me be your banker instead of Pitborough and Orde's, and in that way forget about it?"

"Thank you, Mr Pitborough, you mean to be kind I daresay." The youngster drew himself up with pride that made the banker realize ruefully that he was dealing with a member of an old and aristocratic family, whatever the condition of his finances might be. "I am not accustomed to forgetting my debts."

"But what is the use of starving yourself over such a trifling matter?" Charles was vexed. "You are not looking nearly as well as when you were living with old Mrs Chadwell. You are starving yourself to pay the bank a trifling debt, which I would far rather you made a personal one to myself—as a friend."

"My salary is ample for my needs," said the boy obstinately.

"I'm glad to hear it." Charles Pitborough wondered how he found a salary of ninety pounds a year ample for his needs. It was true that he started off his young bank clerks at this salary, but only after assuring himself that either they lived at home, or their fathers were able to help them by supplying a small additional income. "Then will you accept the invitation of a friend, if you will not accept ten pounds of his money?" he asked mildly.

"That depends upon what it is."

"What a prickly customer you are! I want you to come to Italy with me at the end of May and be my guest there for a fortnight," Charles said. "I do not want to be alone, and some friends of mine in Milchester will be visiting Venice at that time."

"Venice?" The boy frowned. "But I have already lost a month of my salary over this wretched accident, and I do not see how I can afford to lose another fortnight on a holiday. I have never had a holiday in my life."

"Which is all the more reason why you should take one now. You have just said that your salary is ample for your needs, but if these needs are met from another source for fortnight or so you will not miss it, will you? And as I have a sister who married an Italian some years ago and will no doubt be in Venice during June in an enormous palazzo big enough to house a regiment, I will persuade her to take us in as her guests, so that you need not feel you are running into debt on my account."

"And our travelling expenses?" said Mr Tilverton mildly. "I conclude that you are not thinking of walking to Italy?"

"These things can be undertaken very inexpensively." Mr Pitborough brushed it aside. "I believe my friend Mr Lavender made his arrangements through the admirable Thomas Cook."

"Lavender?" repeated Barnaby thoughtfully. "And from Milchester you said?"

"Yes. It is an uncommon name. He and his wife

are going on a trip to Italy, taking their very pretty daughter with them. Oh, don't mistake me. My interest is not in the young lady."

Barnaby's thoughts went back to Love Lane and to Rosalind, running down the lane to meet him, the blue spring sky reflected in the puddles left by a passing shower, the sunshine on her face and in her eyes. Her little dog, her chatter, their sudden silences when there was no need to speak because they knew they were in love. He drew a deep breath.

"I ought not to accept your invitation," he said. "But I will be happy to do so. I shall repay your kindness to me one day, Mr Pitborough, I can promise you that as sincerely as I promise that I will repay my present debt to the bank before we leave."

"I am glad that is settled then," said Charles. "And now as the day is fine we may as well take the cab that I trust is still waiting below and visit one of those grand hotels in Northumberland Avenue for luncheon."

* * * * *

William Pitborough said he was delighted to hear that old Charles was proposing to take a holiday. "You work too hard," he told him. "And I shall be here to take charge."

That was the only thing that really bothered Charles Pitborough.

6

May the 30th marked the end of the Lavenders' visit
to Switzerland and the two girls were sitting under
the umbrellas of the chestnut trees on the Strand at
Lucerne while Cecily put some finishing touches to
a sketch she had been making of Pilatus rising above
the lake, when Mr Ferndean returned from his walk
with Mr Lavender.

He had been their companion for the past week
while they were in Switzerland and Cecily had found
him a dull young man and secretly sympathized with
Rosalind when she made no secret of the fact that he
bored her.

"We had a most interesting walk," he told them, a
piece of information that Rosalind received without
enthusiasm. Cecily was more polite and remarked that
it had been a fine morning for it. "The weather has
been kind to you for your last day," she added. "Do

you start back for England this afternoon, Mr Ferndean?"

"No, I shall take the overnight express. The European trains are very comfortable, and it will give me a little more time with you all." He smiled placatingly at his beloved. "How have you enjoyed Switzerland, Rosalind?"

"I have not enjoyed it at all," she said crossly. "I am sick and tired of mountains. I have walked up them and down them, I have gazed at them in the sunset, and I was even dragged up one morning at three o'clock to see the sunrise. I have been round them on lake steamers, and I have been up one of them in a dreadful mountain railway, which terrified me. Yes, you may laugh, Mr Ferndean, but I am not at all convinced that it was safe and neither was anybody else. Suppose anything had given way? We should all have been thrown to the bottom and probably into the lake."

He explained rather ponderously the mechanics of the railway in question that made such an eventuality impossible but she remained unconvinced, and at last he had to yield to her over the mountains, adding, "But if you have not liked Switzerland, you must have enjoyed Paris?"

"That I did not then." She was still cross. "Do you know how many people there were in that tour we joined, Mr Ferndean? Over fifty, with one guide rounding us up as if he was a sheep dog and we were a flock of sheep. It was like going about in a menagerie, wasn't it, Cecily? We were taken to picture galleries and we could not get near the pictures because of our fellow tourists, and we went on an excursion to

Versailles, which Papa thought such a good idea because Mamma and Cecily and I would not be confined to our hotel while he was busy with his business friends in Paris. But we would far rather have had an opportunity of visiting the Paris shops, wouldn't we, Cis?"

Cecily could not agree there. "You are a Philistine, Rosalind," she said. "There are shops to be found everywhere, but there is only one Notre-Dame and only one Palace of Versailles. I must say I enjoyed seeing Paris, even with a crowd of other people."

"And such people!" Rosalind was unwilling to yield an inch.

"Oh come, Rosalind, some of them were very nice." Cecily laughed. "I do not know why you are in such a bad temper this morning. Don't you remember that dear old clergyman and his son and daughter-in-law? He had never been out of England in his life because he was too poor, and when a rich parishioner died and left him some money he took his family to see Paris and the Swiss mountains."

"He was welcome to them," said Rosalind, but the cloud left her face and she laughed too.

"Surely there were not as many as fifty in your party here?" said Mr Ferndean.

"Oh, we left half of them behind in Paris," said Rosalind. "And tomorrow we start out by ourselves for Italy and for Venice—a most romantic city. Is it not romantic, Mr Ferndean?"

The poor man wanted to tell her that any city where she was would be a romantic one for him, but he could not say it in front of Cecily. Instead he admired Miss Floyd's painting and asked Rosalind if she had done any sketches too.

"No. I can't paint as well as Cis does. It would be nice if I could, but I can't."

"You could if you tried," protested Cecily. "And then you would be able to take home something better than wooden candlesticks carved with eidelweiss and brass cow bells with a patron saint for a handle." She began to put away her paints and brushes, studying the sketch critically. It was years since she had had time in which to paint and although the little picture was only the work of an amateur she thought it would serve to remind her of the mountains and the sunshine and warmth of that morning with Rosalind sitting beside her teasing Mr Ferndean and the lake and the swans beyond. It would all be there when she looked at her picture.

"If it is time to go back to the hotel for luncheon," Rosalind said, "I will give my breakfast toast to the swans." She got up and walked away to the lakeside and Mr Ferndean followed her.

Cecily had not been in Paris a day before Mrs Lavender had found an opportunity for a little chat with her while they were waiting for Rosalind to join them one morning. She did so hope that Miss Floyd might be able to persuade Rosalind to regard Mr Ferndean in a more favourable light. It was so good for dearest Ros to have a sensible girl like Miss Floyd for her friend, and her mother knew that she always paid a great deal of attention to what she said. When Mr Ferndean joined them at Lucerne she did trust that the romance of the mountains would make Rosalind kinder to him.

Poor Mr Ferndean, and the poor Lavenders. It

was a pity that Rosalind had taken such a strong dislike to the romantic mountains.

At times however Cecily became a little puzzled as to what part she was expected to play in the party. Before Mr Ferndean's arrival, Mrs Lavender would be nodding her head at her to go and separate Rosalind from some of the younger tourists, whose male members were inclined to be boisterous, if not downright familiar, from catching a girl round the waist while helping her up steep paths, to encouraging her to jump into their arms on the way down. But after Mr Ferndean's arrival Rosalind's mother would be nodding at her friend to join her and her husband and to leave Rosalind with her admirer, a proceeding that Rosalind resisted by holding tightly on to Cecily's arm and refusing to let her go. Cecily wondered what Mrs Lavender would have said if she had known of the letter that she had given her daughter from young Mr Tilverton. Sometimes she wondered uneasily if she ought to have given it to her: it had sent the colour to Rosalind's face when she had read it, and she had laughed over it and dashed away a tear, and she thought that Barnaby Tilverton was the most wonderful as well as the most persecuted person in the whole world, and that directly she returned home she intended to seek out Mrs Chadwell and to ask for his address in London so that she could write to him. Which was all rather worrying for her young duenna.

The party of tourists with whom they had travelled had gone and the dining-room seemed empty without them, although Rosalind said unkindly that she had been pleased to see them go.

"Now, Rosalind," said her mother reprovingly, "you

know you made friends with several young ladies. I
heard you promising to write to two of them before
they left."

"Oh, but I never write letters," said Rosalind. "I
leave that to Cecily. I think she has written to her
family nearly every day, haven't you, Cis?"

Cecily said that there had been so many things to
tell them that she felt she had to write frequently. Her
conscience too had been somewhat appeased by writing often to her mother, and took some of the sting
from Mrs Floyd's accusations of selfishness.

That afternoon they had a last trip on the lake
steamer and Cecily obeyed Mrs Lavender's nods and
stayed with her and Mr Lavender while Mr Ferndean
took possession of Rosalind on a seat by the rail,
pointing out certain aspects of the mountains that
might have escaped her. She was a great deal kinder
to him that afternoon, perhaps a little bit ashamed of
her behaviour, because after all he had come a long
way to be with her for a week.

"I don't know why he makes a good barrister," she
had told Cecily as they got ready for the trip that
afternoon. "But perhaps all good barristers are dull
to their families and their friends? It may be that they
use up their wits in the court-room and have nothing
left when they are free. I should not like to marry a
barrister—or a judge."

Cecily did not think it likely that she would marry a
judge. "But do be a little kinder to poor Mr Ferndean," she added. "As it is his last afternoon with you
for some time."

"It will only make him propose again," said Rosalind gloomily. "But as he does that if I am *not* kind to

him it doesn't matter very much. I wish he would take no for an answer. It would make us all so much happier!"

But it seemed that Mr Ferndean did not take no for an answer and seated at the rail with Rosalind on the lake steamer he once more asked her to marry him and once more she refused him.

"You know," she said to Cecily that night after he had departed in a dejected mood to catch the night train to Paris, "Mrs Blades was quite wrong when she said that travel broadened the mind. It has not broadened Giles Ferndean's mind one little bit."

* * * * *

Charles Pitborough wrote to his sister in Italy saying that he proposed to visit her in Venice, bringing his small daughter and Barnaby Tilverton with him. *I suppose*, he wrote, *Enrico will be opening up that dilapidated old ruin of his on the Grand Canal again this June, which means that the Pudding's cousins will be there. I have warned my man Rigby to keep his hands off Italian bottoms. Mrs Bolingbroke had to reprimand him lately over his behaviour with a new housemaid—a plump country girl, whose buxom charms appealed to the old sinner.*

His sister Miriam telegraphed back that they would be delighted to see them all, and only his aunt was shocked at the idea of such a journey for her greatniece and her nurse.

"Nurse Appleby does not know what to take and what to leave behind," she complained. "I have advised her to take chlorodyne for stomach upsets, grey powders for constipation, Keating's Powder for bed bugs, and ammonia for mosquito bites."

"I trust we shall not need Keating's in Miriam's palazzo."

"But you have to get there first," she pointed out. "Even if the Contessa's house is free from bed bugs, hotels may not be. And what clothes is she to pack for the child, Nurse wants to know? French silk dresses or serge? Or Holland smocks for hot weather?"

"Oh let her take what she has got," said Charles impatiently. "We can buy anything else she needs when we are in Venice. It is a civilized city after all."

"*No* foreign city is civilized," said his aunt, lugubriously. "Goodness knows what Rigby will be like with all those foreign hussies to lead him on. And there is another thing that is troubling me about this trip of yours. I do not think that you ought to leave the bank for so long."

"Now what do you mean by that?" He spoke with rising exasperation and she shook her head at him reprovingly.

"It is no good taking that tone with me, Charles. You know quite well what I mean. Your father would *never* have left the bank in the hands of anyone as irresponsible as your cousin William. I think you should ask Joseph Orde to come and take charge. He is the Senior Partner after all."

"Uncle Joseph came down from Lancashire for the monthly meeting a couple of weeks ago, and his next visit is not due until the end of June, and I shall be back long before then. I do not want him here while I am away as he has a habit of making disastrous decisions, while William will make no decisions at all, but will simply shelve all problems until I return. If there should be any sudden difficulty he knows he has only to telegraph me and I shall be home in four days."

"H'm," said his aunt. "A great deal can happen in four days. What I cannot understand is why you feel you must go. I know you say it is because you want to give Mr Tilverton a holiday, which is very good of you I'm sure. Not that his uncle will thank you for it—you won't curry any favour in that quarter I promise you. But to leave the bank with William in charge is incomprehensible to me. I don't think I remember your father ever leaving the bank in his life—except occasionally from a Friday to a Monday. He would never have dreamed of it."

"My father's circumstances were rather different from mine," said Charles.

"At least he made enough money to buy this house," his aunt reminded him. "And to leave you, his only son, sufficient to keep you in luxury that even the Contessa's husband cannot equal." The old lady always referred to her married niece in Italy by her title, being somewhat contemptuous of it as being foreign and therefore suspect. "You would not like to telegraph to your Uncle Herbert to come?"

"I would not." His Uncle Herbert was in the States again and not likely to be home until Christmas.

"Then I will go to bed, and if anything happens to the bank while you are away you will not be able to say that I did not warn you."

"I would not dare to say it, Aunt Hannah." He kissed her good night with a half-smile and again she shook her head at him reproachfully as she kissed him in return.

"I believe you are up to something," she told him.

"And I wish I knew what it was."

Charles was pleased that she did not.

The Oatesby estate was a large one and worth a great deal of money, but Charles Pitborough did not attach the same importance to it as his father had done and as his aunt did now. If he had ever had a son to hand it to it might have been different, but his married life had been such a disaster that afterwards his house and his fortune had mattered nothing.

7

Three days later Mr and Mrs Lavender and the two girls were in Venice, having travelled through the Alps all the way by train, the ladies overruling Mr Lavender's suggestion that they should take a diligence through some of the more renowned of the mountain passes. The sunshine on the snow-capped ranges against a deep blue sky, however, coupled with the wealth of wild flowers that tumbled down the mountainsides to the track, drew forth exclamations of delight from them all, even Rosalind.

They arrived in Venice in the afternoon to find a fleet of gondolas waiting to meet the train, and several being attached to the Great Britain Hotel they soon found one to take them there, the gondoliers eager to point out the best-known of the palazzos as they made their way up the Grand Canal.

Mr Lavender, who had purchased a *Baedeker's*

Guide to Italy before he left England, regarded the information they gave with sceptism, but Cecily and Rosalind were more gullible, and that night Cecily wrote to her uncle while it was fresh in her mind: *You can have no idea how wonderful it was, gliding up the Grand Canal in that romantic little black craft between the great houses that they call palaces. And indeed they are very like palaces to me. The mooring posts in front of each house are painted in the colours of the family's escutcheon, and over most of the great doorways are coats of arms. Some of the smaller houses are in the possession of English and American people. Mr Robert Browning's house—where he died last December—and Sir Harry Mendip's, and of course the house where Byron lived, were all pointed out to us. Oh, and we saw too the palazzo belonging to your friend, Sir Frederick Rand. It was like travelling through a fairy city. I am afraid Mr and Mrs Lavender were not equally impressed however. Mr Lavender was anxious about our luggage, following in a second gondola, and Mrs Lavender sad she was afraid the houses must be damp to live in, and that some of them looked to be in very poor condition. My love to Mamma and the family, Your loving Cecily.*

Mr Lavender had other things to occupy his mind besides the safe arrival of their luggage, however, and he paid scant attention to their surroundings. He told his companions that in the morning he would take his guidebook and show them all there was to be seen on their own, without any help from foreigners.

"I have been warned against so-called *'valets de places'*," he said. "Many will charge exorbitantly and do not know the half of what they are talking about any more than the gondoliers."

"I hope our hotel has supplied us with mosquito netting for our beds," worried Mrs Lavender. "Mrs Blades told me that if they had not done so we will be able to obtain it from chemists in Venice, but I am sure the girls and I do not want to spend our first evening sewing up our mosquito nets before we dare light our bedroom candles."

"Mrs Blades also warned you that we should keep our bedroom windows closed at night," Rosalind reminded her, and made a little face. "I do not think I shall like that—it is very hot here, isn't it, although it is already late in the afternoon."

Her spirits, somewhat dampened since they left Lucerne by her parents' disapproval of her treatment of Mr Ferndean, had been rising steadily on the journey. Venice, she felt, without the prospect of another visit from her persistent lover, was a great deal more romantic than the mountains. While Cecily, as she watched the sparkling sea washing the quayside where the creamy walls of the Doge's Palace rose above it, agreed that Venice was indeed a romantic city. She could understand English poets settling there, and it made her feel a completely different person from the practical and sensible girl who had looked after her family so assiduously over the past few years. Practical common sense had no place in this beautiful city, rising from the sea. It was totally impractical and full of dreams and washed with history as legendary as fairy tales.

Certainly Mr Lavender was not going to be put off with any airy fancies of romance. For the next two

days he conducted the ladies sternly from the Doge's
Palace to St Mark's and on through galleries, museums and churches, guide-book in hand, careful that
nothing should escape them.

And then one afternoon during the siesta hour
when it was said in Italy that only dogs and English
tourists ventured out, Lady Rand's gondola brought
her to call upon Mr and Mrs Lavender and to make
the acquaintance of Miss Floyd, the General having
written some weeks previously to tell his old friends
of his niece's arrival. A cheerful little body, with a
matter-of-fact air that reminded Cecily of Mrs Blades,
she told her that she was very much like her uncle,
hoped that it was not too warm for them all, and invited them to dinner at half past eight on the following
evening. And then she went away.

Mr Lavender felt that eight-thirty was a late hour
for his digestion, and he was very much afraid that
there would be Italian food and cooking in Sir Frederick's house. Italian cooking did not agree with him
and it was because the Great Britain Hotel served
English food cooked in the English way to its guests
that he had selected it. Mrs Lavender had been disappointed that afternoon tea was not served in a
winter garden as was done in so many Continental
hotels to cater for their English visitors, but her husband said you could not expect foreigners to think of
everything.

Sir Frederick Rand's palazzo, they discovered, small
as it was by Venetian standards, followed the pattern
of the larger ones. There was the entrance from the
Grand Canal into a square courtyard, where servants
waited to show them up a wide staircase to the

rooms on the first floor where the family lived—spacious and deliciously cool rooms with their marble floors bare of carpets.

Sir Frederick had been a great game hunter in his youth, and trophies reflecting his prowess adorned the walls, furniture and floors of his house. There were boars' heads and rhinoceros's heads in between deer's antlers on the walls, and leopard skins draped settees, and tiger and lion skins, the heads mounted to trap the unwary, were spread about the floors. Elephants' feet were mounted to become umbrella stands, and a stuffed grizzly bear became a stand to take gentlemen's hats, while carved ivory tusks decorated the walls or became paper-knives on writing tables. It seemed that no creature in the animal kingdom had been safe from Sir Frederick's guns. Mr Lavender looked about him with interest as he delivered his hat to the grizzly bear: he wished he had had the opportunities to collect such trophies. A deer's head with those large antlers would look imposing in his hall in Tilverton Crescent.

A good few people seemed to be in the salon when they arrived, but the numbers that would have crowded Mrs Lavender's drawing-room were as nothing in that large and airy room. At one end there was a balcony with a painted roof, overlooking the Canal, and at the other windows looked down on a charming garden with statues gleaming white between oleander trees. Cecily and Rosalind made their way towards these windows and were looking down on the garden with delight, while Mr Lavender was beginning to wonder how much longer his digestion would have to wait for his dinner, when the last guests arrived,

an Italian countess whose name they did not catch
and two gentlemen with her.

Rosalind happened to turn back from the window
at that moment, and seeing the fair-haired young
Englishman who was being greeted by their hostess,
gave a little gasp and turned so white that Cecily
thought she felt faint.

"What is the matter, Ros?" she asked in a low voice.
"Is it the heat?"

"No. Look who just came into the room, Cis."
Cecily followed the direction of her friend's eyes, but
it was the fair-haired young man's companion that
drew her startled gaze far more than the object of
Rosalind's interest. What on earth, she thought, was
Mr Charles Pitborough doing in Venice?

With the last time they had met in Tilverton Park
clear in her mind she hoped that she would be able
to avoid him in the crowd in the room, but at that
moment dinner was announced and Lady Rand was
gathering her guests together and she had to leave
the shelter of the window.

It seemed obvious to the kindly lady that the two
English girls with the Lavenders should have English-
men for their partners, and she asked Charles to take
Cecily in and handed Rosalind over to Barnaby Tilverton. The Lavenders were a little more difficult to
place, but she had invited a little English spinster living in Venice for Mr Lavender, and gave Mrs Lavender to the tender mercies of an English clergyman,
who manged to steer their conversation adroitly into
describing the many Venetian charities to which kind-
hearted tourists generously contributed when they
visited the city.

It is feared that Mr and Mrs Lavender paid no more than a polite attention to their partners, their minds being centred on their daughter, who was blossoming like a rose, her eyes sparkling, her lips smiling, as she talked to young Mr Tilverton with an animation and ease that poor Mr Ferndean had never received at her hands. Mr Lavender's digestion suffered severely that night.

Cecily found no such delight in her partner. She saw the quick look of appreciation that he gave her golden dress, but if he was surprised by the metamorphis of the dowdy Miss Floyd he gave no sign of it. He offered her his arm in silence, and having placed the tips of her fingers on his sleeve as he conducted her into dinner she was thankful to reclaim them as they sat down at the long English mahogany table in the dining-room.

"Are you staying long in Venice, Miss Floyd?" he asked as she seemed disinclined to start any sort of conversation.

"Three weeks," she said briefly. "And you? I was astonished to see you here, Mr Pitborough. I presume you are on business?"

"Partly." For a second his eyes met hers and she fancied she saw a glint of humour in them which made her drop her own swiftly to her plate.

"And your daughter?" she asked hastily. "I hope she was well when you left?"

"She is with me," he told her. "My sister's Italian husband has a palazzo here in Venice, and a country estate near Florence, and while Enrico prefers the country at this time of year my sister insists that their old palazzo must be lived in for some months in each year or else it will fall into the Canal. And as she objects to wintering here when thick white fogs come up out of the sea to envelop the city giving it a chilly, not to say eerie atmosphere, and July and August are too hot, she usually stays only for May and June. She has brought her three children with her this year, and it seemed an excellent opportunity for Janie to be introduced to her cousins."

"How do they get on together?" Question and answer she felt might be the least embarrassing mode of conversation between them.

"Very well, fortunately."

"Do your sister's children speak English?"

"Oh, yes. They have an English nurse, otherwise I would not have dared to bring Nurse Appleby all this way. They speak Italian as well, and Janie is picking up a few words here and there."

"And where do they play?"

"There is a large nursery at the top of the house, and my sister has a garden rather larger than Sir Frederick's here. There are a surprising number of gardens in Venice."

"I have noticed that." She became slightly less frigid. "Quite often as one passes a garden wall one can smell roses and orange blossom."

"A better smell than that of the canals," he said gravely and again as she glanced at him he thought she almost smiled. At all events something trembled for a moment at the corner of her mouth and it was remarkably like a smile. He turned quickly to the city's treasures: what had they seen as yet and what did they intend to see tomorrow?

She was glad to enthuse over the Doge's Palace,

thought she was boring him and was pleased to continue because in that case he would not be likely to pursue the conversation after dinner.

The gentlemen did not follow the English custom of staying in the dining-room and lingering over port wine and brandy after the ladies had retired to the drawing-room, however. They went back with them to the salon where conversation became general and the Rands circulated among their guests, breaking up little groups of Italians and giving them the doubtful pleasure of listening to unintelligible Italian from English friends and hazarding equally unintelligible English of their own in reply. When she felt she had done enough to make them entertain each other Lady Rand left them to recover from the polite exhaustion that was attacking them and suggested that they should have some music, indicating the large grand piano in a corner of the room.

"Now who will play accompaniments?" she asked.

"You had better ask my brother," the Contessa said. "He plays better than anybody I know."

"Mr Pitborough?" Lady Rand was delighted and led him to the piano at once. Cecily regarded his segregation with satisfaction as it seemed likely that she was to be relieved from the business of avoiding him for the rest of the evening, but her satisfaction was short-lived.

"And who," continued Lady Rand, smiling once more on her assembled guests, "will be so kind as to entertain us with a few English songs?"

Cecily looked about her for Rosalind, who had suddenly disappeared, and she was horrified to hear Charles Pitborough say in his decided way, "I am sure Miss Floyd knows a number of songs."

"Miss Floyd. The very one!" Lady Rand approached her affectionately. "It is such a pleasure to have you here, my dear! Please give us a song."

She did not feel able to refuse, but she did not forgive Mr Pitborough, and as she joined him at the piano she was determined to find fault with everything he selected.

Some were too high for her voice, she said, and some were too low: some were too difficult for her to attempt, and some she did not know at all.

Finally he unearthed a book of ballads. "Come," he said good-naturedly, "before I despair of finding anything among Lady Rand's music to suit you, look through these and do not tell me that you have never sung 'Auld Robin Gray' or 'Comin' Thro' the Rye,' or 'Caller Herrin', because if you do I shall not believe you."

Reluctantly she chose the last two he named and she found that she was singing better than usual. Her accompanist did not drown her voice as Rosalind was apt to do at home, and his touch was sensitive and fine, so that she could feel that she had a partner in her songs and not an opponent as was so often the case in Milchester drawing-rooms.

It was not an exhibition that she enjoyed and as the company applauded and asked for just one more her annoyance with the man who gravely added his request to the rest increased.

She leafed through the book and finally put it in front of him, open at a song. "I'll sing that," she said, "it is nice and short."

To her surprise he sat for a moment with his hands

in front of him, all expression gone from his face, and at first she thought he was going to refuse to play, and then abruptly he shut the book and put it aside. "I do not need the music," he said.

His hands touched the keys lightly, waiting for her voice, and she sang the old song plaintively:

> "Early one morning, just as the sun was rising,
> I heard a maid sing in the valley below,
> Oh, don't deceive me, Oh never leave me!
> How could you use a poor maiden so?"

As she sang she happened to glance across the room and saw the Contessa's face, startled, compassionate, concerned for her brother, and suddenly she was sorry for the ill-humour that had made her select that particular song. Maybe it had memories for the man at the piano, and the cold almost inhuman Charles Pitborough had feelings, after all. When she had finished she thanked him for his accompaniment, put the book away, and once more she looked about her again for Rosalind

But Rosalind was out on the balcony with the painted roof, and young Mr Tilverton was with her, and once more they had forgotten everything but each other.

As she got ready for bed that night Mrs Lavender said in pleased tones to her husband, "That nice Contessa!—I thought it was so kind of her to ask us in to tea tomorrow. 'I know you are longing for an Enlish tea,' she said. "Well, to be honest with you, Contessa,' I said. 'I am. I have not tasted a good cup of tea since I left England.' She broke off. 'I have not seen Mr Pitborough so friendly either. At home he always seems such a cold sort of man. He told me that some of the pictures in his sister's palazzo are well worth seeing. I had no idea he played the piano, had you?"

"I did not think you need have asked his friend, young Tilverton, to join us tomorrow," said her husband, disregarding Mr Pitborough's performance at the piano. "I do not want that young man encouraged to run after Rosalind, my dear. I don't forget that he danced four dances with her at the Palace ball, and he was out on the balcony with her for quite some time tonight. I do not like it. He has no money and no prospects and what is more he is very unpopular with his uncle Lord Tilverton."

"I asked him to join us, my dear," said Mrs Lavender, smiling, "because I intend to stop it at once."

"What do you mean?" Mr Lavender gave a belch. "Stop what?"

"Any fancy he may have about Rosalind, and any fancies she may have about him," said Mrs Lavender firmly, and, still smiling, she got into bed.

"Where have you put the peppermint?" asked the long-suffering Mr Lavender. As he had feared the Rands employed an Italian cook and garlic coupled with everything cooked in oil did not agree with his English stomach.

8

It is annoying when you have spent most of the night collecting weapons with which to fight a person, to find when morning comes that he will not be there to fight. Cecily, who had composed withering replies to anything that Mr Pitborough might offer in the way of conversation the following day was put out because only Mr Tilverton turned up to accompany them on their tour of sightseeing that day, his friend being engaged with his sister. She found herself walking ahead with Mr Lavender and his guide-book and Rosalind and perversely missing Charles Pitborough's challenging astringency.

Mrs Lavender walked more slowly behind them with Mr Tilverton. "I find these Italian pavements cruel to my feet. Mr Tilverton." said Rosalind's mother, "I can't walk as fast as the two girls. But I know you will not mind giving me your arm."

Gallantly he gave her his arm: was not his adorable Rosalind her daughter?

"I expect Rosalind has told you about Mr Ferndean." Mrs Lavender stopped to rearrange the veil on her hat. "The sun is so fierce this morning," she complained. "Though we start out as early as ten o'clock it is surprising how warm it can be at that hour in these southern countries. And I am so afraid of mosquitos."

"I don't remember Miss Lavender mentioning Mr Ferndean," said Barnaby slowly, holding her sunshade while she put the veil right.

"Well, I daresay she would not," said Mrs Lavender archly. "After all, it is a secret as yet." She waited for this to take effect before she continued, "I know you will not tell her that I have told you, but, you see, she is unofficially engaged to Mr Ferndean. Such a nice man—and so clever. A rising young barrister who shows a great deal of promise, so we are told, and, of course, with large private means. Nobody can be a barrister without considerable private means, and I can promise you, Mr Tilverton," with a little laugh, "the man who marries Rosalind will need a good income. She is an extravagant little puss. He proposed to her at Lucerne—he spent a week with us before we came on to Italy—but she wanted it kept a secret because—well, girls are a bit shy over things like that. When we get home no doubt he will meet her with an engagement ring, and all we shall have to do then will be to fix the date of the wedding. But please keep it a secret, won't you, Mr Tilverton? She would never forgive me if she knew I had told you about it."

Mr Tilverton assured her in a somewhat hollow

voice that he would indeed keep it a secret.

"There!" said Mrs Lavender brightly. "My veil is all right now. I will take my sunshade from you again. Thank you so much, Mr Tilverton, for bearing so kindly with an old woman's slowness."

"There is no hurry, Mrs Lavender. No hurry in the world." And as he handed her the holland sunshade with its green lining, poor Barnaby felt that indeed there was no hurry to join Rosalind now that he knew she belonged to another.

"That horrid girl," the Contessa said to her brother when he joined her for rolls and coffee that morning in the palazzo garden.

"What horrid girl?" He put on his blandest expression and she could have shaken him.

"The girl who sang that song last night at the Rands," she said sharply. "Gussie's song."

"But she was not to know that," he replied reasonably.

"Are you sure she did not know? I caught her looking at you once or twice during dinner as if she hated you."

"I cannot help her looks, and I give her full permission to hate me if she pleases." He sounded as if it was a most desirable state of affairs. "I do not remember having asked for her affection." He helped himself to a roll, spread it with honey, and ate it with an appetite. "I never can get used to your Continental breakfasts, Miriam, but there is no denying that they are delicious."

His sister gave it up. She knew that when he was in this mood he would tell her nothing. She asked instead, "Will you be in this afternoon when your friends come

to tea?" She laid a slight emphasis on the word
"friends" and he frowned.

"I thought you wished me to obtain some tickets
for the theatre tonight?"

"One of the servants can be sent for them."

"Can they be trusted to know what you like?"

"I daresay they cannot. Very well. In that case I
give you permission to get the tickets yourself and
miss my tea party."

He seemed relieved that the matter had been settled
so easily and as the nurses arrived at that moment with
the children he stayed to finish his breakfast and to
improve his acquaintance with Janie's cousins.

The tea party that afternoon was rated a success by
the ladies, who went to it alone, Mr Lavender being
detained by his digestion. The tea was as English
as a cup of tea without milk could be, and the cakes
as English as Italian cooks could make them, and
after tea, in the English fashion, the children came
down from the nursery in their party clothes to say
"how do you do" to the Contessa's guests. Her own
children, two girls and a little boy, stood in a group
rather too shy to make friends, but Janie had no in-
hibitions and made friends with everyone, and finally
came to a halt beside Cecily and told her that she
knew her.

"You are Miss Floyd," she said gravely. "Bella's
sister at the dancing class, and you helped me button
my boots because Nurse was so slow and I couldn't
get them buttoned up and Papa was waiting with the
dog-cart and I was afraid he would go without me."

"Nurse did her best," Cecily reminded her, smiling.
"But you were in too much of a hurry."

"I was so afraid Papa would go," explained Janie again.

"But surely you knew he would not? He had told you that he would wait for you, I think."

The Contessa looked at her quickly with awakened interest. Could Charles have met this girl over Janie's dancing class? But if so, why had he said nothing about it? Could Cecily Floyd's presence here be the reason for his sudden holiday in Venice? She must watch him more closely—and yet when he came in later with his friend young Tilverton he scarcely looked at Cecily: his bow to the ladies included her with the rest.

The Contessa could not understand it. She asked him if he had been successful in obtaining theatre tickets and he said that he had.

"How many did you get?" she asked.

"Seven. Three for ourselves and four for Mr Lavender's party. I believe you wished to include them did you not?"

"Certainly," she said smiling, not revealing that the purchase of the extra tickets was as much a surprise to her as it was to them. "I will send one of the gondolas for them at nine. I hope your husband will join us, Mrs Lavender. The Fenice is our best theatre, but alas it is seldom open, and through in the winter we manage a little opera here—generally excrutiatingly performed—in June few of the remaining theatres are open. I see that these tickets are for the Malibran: that is the one on a little canal that joins the Grand Canal near the Rialto Bridge, so that it will not be out of the way."

Mrs Lavender said that she was sure they would

enjoy it very much. "I enjoyed the French theatres we went to in Paris," she added. "My husband said it was probably a good thing that I could not understand the language for some of the plays, but neither could he, and he enjoyed it as much as the girls and I did."

Charles Pitborough saw the girls exchange quick glances and from the repressed mirth in their faces he thought that probably they had understood a great deal more than their seniors.

They all enjoyed the theatre that night, however, and afterwards they found a small fleet of gondolas waiting in the little canal to take them back to their hotel, and to her chagrin and embarrassment Cecily found herself alone in one of them with Charles Pitborough.

"I wanted this opportunity of speaking to you," he said, as they moved out into midstream after the others. "You will remember no doubt, the proposition I made to you before you left Milchester, and your reply?"

"Yes, Mr Pitborough," she said, vexed with the manoeuvering that had got her into the gondola with him. "I remember."

"I wrote to your uncle and I believe he showed you my letter, or told you of its contents, because I had a reply from him saying that you would discuss the matter further with me on your return to England."

His quiet voice accused her of ungraciousness and she said quickly, "I would have written to you myself, but there was no time. I was leaving in a few hours."

"So the General said in his letter." He was looking

ahead of him as they came out into the Grand Canal, sitting forward with his hands lightly clasped in front of him, and the light from the gondola's lantern falling on his face. It showed it to be thoughtful and grave, and, with the arrogance momentarily gone, it was a fine face and a sensitive one. "That is why I am here. When I make up my mind to a thing I do not like to be kept waiting months for a reply, Miss Floyd." The slight smile that accompanied the words failed to reassure her.

The General had told her that he did not think Mr Pitborough was a man to be lightly thwarted, and it seemed that he had been right. She said steadily: "I cannot believe that you came all this way just to discuss the proposition you made to me. Mr Pitborough."

He looked faintly surprised. "But that is precisely the case," he said. "First of all I want to know why it is so important to you to have your family with you at Oatesby—apart from family ties and natural affection and that sort of thing." He brushed such things aside contemptuously and she flushed with indignation.

"Mr Pitborough," she said coldly, "affection for my family has nothing to do with it. If I had been a man," here she paused long enough for him to put in ironically:

"My dear young lady, if you had been a man the situation would not have arisen, would it? But that is by the way. Please continue."

"If I had been a man," she went on frostily, "I would have been able to make a home for my family, directly I could earn enough to keep them, so that they could live with me and be my responsibility alone. But as I am a woman such prospects are denied me, and the next best thing is for me to marry a rich man and provide for them in that way."

He seemed to be surprised, as if this aspect of the situation had not occurred to him. Then, "You sound remarkably cold-blooded," he remarked drily, and she saw that he was frowning.

"It is because of my uncle," she said, impatient with him for his lack of understanding, and went on in a quieter tone: "Before we came, my dear Uncle Humphrey lived a contented and happy bachelor existence. He hunted twice a week in the winter, he fished in the summer, and on one night a week throughout the year three of his old cronies would gather at his house for dinner and a game of whist. And once a week he would dine at the Liberal Club. He had his soldier servant Pringle as his butler and groom—my brothers torment the life out of the poor man—and he had his nice housekeeper and three maids and a gardener who would wait on table sometimes. He was most perfectly happy. And then my father died, so heavily in debt that Uncle Humphrey felt he must offer us a home. He gave up his hunters, he gave up his fishing, he no longer entertains his friends, and he does not dine at the Liberal Club any more. And now he is talking of giving up his gig and his gardner, and it's all because of us." Tears sparkled in her eyes. "I feel so—guilty—when I think of his kindness and generosity and the way we have repaid him for it. That is why, when you made your—business proposition—to me, I told you that my family must come with me to Oatesby—for his sake, not for mine. But of course I was wrong. It would not be at all pleasant for you to have them in your home, and I do not see why you, a stranger, should be burdened with my family—or my problems." Her hands tightened on the ivory sticks of the fan in her lap. "So please do not talk of it any more, Mr Pitborough, and please do not waste any more days in Venice because of the stupid things I said to you that day in Tilverton Park. They were largely inspired by caprice." By caprice and by anger because he had shown her how little he thought of her as a woman.

"But you were not being stupid," he said quietly. "And I believe that we might be able to solve your family's problems between us."

She glanced at him in alarm. Did he not see that she did not want to pursue it any further? "Mr Pitborough," she cried, "I do not seem able to make myself clear! I am not the only girl in Milchester. There are many others there who will be ready to marry you if I am not. Of that I am sure."

"I am sure of it too," he said with sublime conceit. "But I happen to have fixed my mind upon you as being the one most suitable for my purpose."

"Suitable as I may be," she said heatedly, "I still do not wish to marry you, and I advise you to find somebody else—without my encumbrances."

"I do not particularly want to find somebody else," he said maddeningly. "And as I said before I think I shall be able to deal with your encumbrances."

"Oh!" she cried, exasperated. "I am afraid you are a very obstinate man."

"I am afraid I am," he agreed, and as the gondola pulled in to the steps that led up to the Great Britain Hotel he got up and held out his hand to help her. She was so angry with him that she did not want to put her hand into his, but she was afraid of slipping, and for a moment his fingers closed tightly on hers. "You had better hold on until we are up the steps," he warned her. "They are confoundedly slippery."

They reached the top and then he released her, continuing to walk with her the few yards to the doorway to the hotel. "Goodbye, Mr Pitborough!" she said with some emphasis.

"Good night, Miss Floyd," he said, correcting her and smiled as he lifted his hat. "I should warn you perhaps that I usually get what I want."

Her eyes met his stormily, "Not *this* time, I think!" she said, and walked into the hotel where the Lavenders were waiting for her.

That night as they undressed in the room they shared, Rosalind said, "Mamma thinks Mr Pitborough is quite struck with you, Cis?"

"Mrs Lavender is quite mistaken," said Cecily.

"Don't you think he might be—just a little bit?"

"I do not."

"That's a pity, because he is so beautifully rich." Rosalind was disappointed. "You don't like him very much, do you?"

"I don't know when I have disliked a man more," said Cecily shortly.

"And that's a pity too, because if he was struck with you and if he asked you to marry him, I cannot imagine that even you—brave as you are—would have the courage to refuse him." Then to Cecily's relief her mind darted off to another subject. "Do you remember that evening in Paris, Cis, when Papa said he was meeting his business friend for dinner? Well, I think he went with him to see the Can-can, because

I heard him tell Mr Pitborough that he found it very disappointing. I wonder what he expected it to be like, don't you? And if it was so tame, why didn't he take us?"

9

The following morning Mr Lavender asked his wife what she had said to Mr Tilverton that had made such a marked difference in his manner towards their daughter.

"Did you tell him that I would not give her a penny if she married a man I did not approve of?" he asked.

"Oh dear no. Nothing like that." Getting out of bed, Mrs Lavender pulled on a loose wrapper with a beaming smile. "I simply told him that she was engaged to Mr Ferndean and that they would be married directly we arrived home. Being a gentleman, doubtless he feels that he can no longer pursue a girl who is engaged to another man."

"It isn't true, though," said her husband, his head emerging from the neck of his shirt like a grizzled Jack-in-the-box. "I don't like the thought of you having told fibs, Martha."

"It worked, all the same," said Mrs Lavender triumphantly. She went to the window and pulled up the wooden blind a few inches. "Lawks Mr L.!" she exclaimed. "Look what's arrived."

Mr Lavender looked, and where there had been an empty, sparkling expanse of sea the day before, now the lagoon held a fleet of grey battleships, "Ironclads!" he cried. "And flying the White Ensign! The Royal Navy, or I'm a Dutchman."

"The fleet is in port," said Mrs Lavender with as much satisfaction as if she had arranged it herself. "That will solve our problems as far as the girls are concerned."

"Why should it affect them?"

"Well, if the British Navy is in port here for a week or so, all the English ladies living in Venice will be trying to outdo each other in entertaining the officers, and they will not need any gentlemen to assist them. It's young ladies the officers will be looking for after six months or so at sea. Our girls will be much in demand, if you ask me."

And after a prolonged scrutiny of the battleships through his telescope later on Mr Lavender pronounced that the ships were certainly British, and that he would not be surprised if she was right.

Certainly her forecast seemed to be correct. The stay of the fleet, they learned, was only to be of short duration, and for the next week every English lady with a palazzo in Venice, from the Consul's wife downwards, invited the officers of the battleships to be her guests at luncheon and dinner and impromptu dances. Rosalind and Cecily were out every evening, and during the day Mr Lavender's guide-book was sadly neglected, and when towards the end of the week the Admiral returned the hospitality that the officers of his flotilla had received by giving a ball on his flagship the *Jupiter*, the Contessa was asked to bring any number of young ladies to it. She sent a note round to Mrs Lavender at once, asking if Rosalind and Cecily could accompany her, and that night at ten her gondola called for them and took them under her chaperonage out to the battleship where the Admiral was receiving his guests.

It was, Cecily and Rosalind declared afterwards, a most hilarious occasion. A ballroom had been made under awnings on deck, an orchestra composed of blue-jackets played all the popular dance tunes of the day from "The Blue Danube" to "The Skaters Waltz," the claret cup was excellent, and with the lights of an enchanted city to gaze at between the dances with partners only too ready to gaze at them instead and be gallantly complimentary, and say with their eyes what words could not say, was enough to sweep the girls off their feet. There were times, Cecily felt, when Rosalind even forgot Mr Tilverton, while as for herself, she was thankful that Mr Pitborough was not there.

When they arrived back at the hotel in the summer dawn, however, with promises to certain officers on board that they had no intention of keeping, it was to dissolve into laughter and to compare rather cruelly the soft nothings of their partners that night and the way they had responded to them.

They agreed before they dropped off to sleep that it was the most delightful ball that they had ever attended and that it would be a long time before they

would forget it. Not for the world would they have
admitted that there had been moments when they
had missed the two men who seemed to avoid their
party since the arrival of the fleet.

Mrs Lavender, calling on the Contessa with the
girls on the following day to thank her for her kindness in taking them, remarked that she understood
that her brother and Mr Tilverton had not been with
them.

"Oh no!" The Contessa smiled. "Men would not
have been welcomed last night, Mrs Lavender, and
Charles would not have attended such an occasion
had he been here. As it happens, he and Mr Tilverton
have been spending this week fishing at Chioggia—or
that is what they said they would be doing!" She
laughed. "But as it is said in Venice that the women
there have always been famed for their beauty and
that, in fact, many of the old painters used to go
to Chioggia for their models, I told them I thought
they were only going to find out for themselves if it
were true." She laughed again with a lightness that
Miss Lavender and Miss Floyd found it hard to
imitate.

"We thought, Mr L. and I," said Mrs Lavender,
with one of her fat comfortable laughs, "that perhaps
the sailors had frightened our gentlemen friends
away."

Cecily's eyes met the Contessa's for a mirthful moment, and she was reminded of one of Lady Scrimgour's crueller moments, when she had said it was a
pity that Mrs Lavender was a rich woman because
she would have made such an excellent housekeeper.

Lady Rand happened to arrive just as they were

leaving, and Mrs Lavender became unexpectedly enthusiastic over Cecily's sketches, bemoaning the fact that she could not go out sketching in Venice as she had done with Rosalind in Lucerne.

"Oh no," said Lady Rand, smiling. "It would not do at all—in fact it would not be safe for two English girls to walk about Venice alone. But if there is a view from any of our windows that you would like to try, Cecily, my dear, you are welcome to come when you like. You know that we shall be delighted to see you."

She added that she would be at home on the following day if her friends could spare her, and Mrs Lavender accepted for her with alacrity. She said it would be a golden opportunity for Cecily to go that day as they intended to visit Murano to look at the glass factory there, which meant a long sea-trip first. "It will probably be a long hot day altogether," she added. "She will be far better off in your cool salon, Lady Rand."

It was not until they were about to start off for their trip on the following day and a good-looking young American turned up with his family to accompany them that Cecily remembered how gushing Mrs Lavender had been to him and to his parents the day before, and she wondered if she had been excluded from the party to Murano so that Rosalind should have no rival with her new admirer.

She was amused by Mrs Lavender's strategems and departed in the Rands' gondola happily with her sketching book, a small portfolio and a folding easel, and her box of paints.

She was very kindly received by her uncle's old

friends, and having decided that the Grand Canal and the palazzos that looked on to it was far too large a subject for her talents, she found that a view from the balcony of the corner of a garden wall next door, where it met the water of a smaller canal, was inviting enough for her to see what she could do. Roses were scrambling over the wall, and ferns were growing in it, and the combination of wall and water and flowers, with a hint of the shuttered windows of a palazzo beyond, kept her happily employed for the morning, while Lady Rand settled herself beside her with her needlework and talked of the days in Malta when they had known the General.

"It is a long time ago now," she told her. "Your mother came out to be his hostess I remember—she was so pretty and everybody admired her so much." Fair-haired, blue-eyed, pretty and spoiled, Lady Rand's thoughts ran, as she watched the sketch growing under Cecily's clever fingers. Her daughter was nothing like her. There had been scores of admirers after Colonel Masterson's pretty sister in those days, and she had married one of the younger officers in his regiment—Captain Floyd. He came from a good family, but had very little money, and she had heard later that Louisa Masterson had helped him run through the little he had. From what Cecily said about her family she gathered that they lived in rather straitened circumstances in Milchester, and she was sorry for the General. She asked if she had heard from home since she had been in Venice and Cecily said she had not, and added wistfully that she supposed letters from England took a long time to arrive.

"I am expecting one from my mother," she said,

"but I daresay it is waiting for me at the Post Office. I have never had my passport with me when we have been sightseeing in that direction."

Wherever she went she was pursued by letters from Mrs Floyd listing complaints: how difficult it had been to get the boys off to school in time in the mornings until the General took a hand and ordered cold baths for them before breakfast, superintended by Pringle. That had cured it, and although Mrs Floyd wrote indignantly to her daughter saying how cruel it was, Cecily could not help feeling that Pringle must have taken an almost sadistic delight in the proceedings, knowing how much the poor man had suffered at her brothers' hands.

The General had also arranged for Bella's governess to stay longer so that she would be available to take her pupil to and from her classes in dancing and music—a most unnecessary expense, Mrs Floyd remarked piously, and one that their dear uncle could well do without.

"I am afraid my family are missing me badly," she told Lady Rand. "I have to harden my heart every time a letter from my mother arrives, or else I would have been off home long ago."

"Then I trust you will control such impulses while you are in Venice," said Lady Rand.

"I am doing my best," Cecily assured her smiling.

It was getting towards lunchtime when Lady Rand was called from the room and after a little while somebody came into it and stood for a moment studying the absorbed artist on the balcony. There were pools of sunlight in the marble floor of the salon, and the dancing reflections from the water gave life to the painted cherubs and their wreaths of flowers on the balcony ceiling. And as his eyes rested on the slender figure sitting there beneath the cherubs for the first time Charles Pitborough allowed himself to admit that Cecily Floyd was an attractive young woman, as well as being the ideal mamma for Janie and a responsible hostess for his house at Oatesby.

He had been uneasily aware of it when he had first seen her at the Palace ball, which was perhaps why he had emphasized the dowdiness of her dress, but every time they had met since had shown him some new facet of her character, so that he had suppressed all feeling about her as firmly as he suppressed it now. He had suffered enough at the hands of a woman, he told himself fiercely: he would allow himself no weakness where women were concerned and he would suffer no more.

After a moment Cecily leant back to study her sketch and said without turning her head, "It is not very good. I'm not an artist I'm afraid."

She heard footsteps crossing the room and then a critical masculine voice observed, "You have talent, all the same. A few lessons might improve it perhaps."

She turned swiftly and the soft pleasure in her face vanished. She closed her paint box. "I beg your pardon," she said, "I thought you were Lady Rand."

"I came with a note from my sister," he said. "Lady Rand is in the writing-room replying to it at this moment. When I have that reply I shall depart." He saw the satisfaction on her face and thought that at least he had nothing to fear from this cool young woman. Far from welcoming his society she looked indecently pleased at the prospect of getting rid of him so quickly.

"Did you enjoy your trip to Chioggia?" she asked coldly.

"Very much, thank you."

"And are the ladies there as good-looking as they are reputed to be?"

"They may be. I am afraid I did not notice. We were out fishing most of the time." He paused. "And you? I hope you enjoyed the Admiral's ball?"

"Oh yes. It was a most brilliant occasion. I have never been to anything like it before."

"And I suppose you and Miss Lavender came home with plenty of scalps hanging from your belts?"

She opened her paint-box again to deepen the outline of a fern on the wall in her picture before replying. Then she said reasonably, "Now, why did you say that?"

"But that is what women enjoy most at a ball, isn't it? To add more scalps to their collections."

She finished the fern before replying and then she said quietly, "The Admiral certainly has some charming young officers on the ships under his command. It was so pleasant to be treated with courtesy and even gallantry—as if one was woman, and not—" again she paused.

"A board meeting?" he suggested wryly. "You need say no more. I know I am culpable." He took up her portfolio and began glancing through it critically. "This one of the mountain is good," he pronounced. "You have got the wisp of cloud round its peak very well."

"That is Pilatus," she told him distantly. "He always

wears that cloud—the local people call it the "tears
of Pilate'."

He refrained from commenting on the eccentricities
of the Swiss, continuing to examine the portfolio in
silence, and then to Cecily's relief Lady Rand came
back with the answer to his sister's letter. "I see you
are admiring Cecily's sketches," she said. "I think she
is very clever, don't you, Mr Pitborough?"

"Talented," he conceded coolly, but when she asked
him to stay to luncheon he refused. He had promised
his sister, he said.

"I was hoping that you might be able to escort
Miss Floyd to the Post Office in her way back to
her hotel this afternoon," said Lady Rand. "She thinks
there may be a letter waiting for her there."

He said he would be happy to return at three
o'clock when the siesta hour was over, and escort her
then.

"It does not matter in the least," Cecily protested,
frowning and put out. "I am sure I can wait until Mr
Lavender goes that way tomorrow. And I have not
got my passport with me today."

"There is no reason why we should not go back
to your hotel, leave your painting things there and
pick up your passport at the same time," said Charles.
"I will be back at three." And he went off with his
sister's letter.

"A strange man, but I think he means kindly," said
Lady Rand when he was gone. "Do you see much of
him in Milchester?"

"I see scarcely anything of him at all," Cecily assured her, making a mental note that in future she
intended to see even less.

Punctually at three o'clock, however, he arrived, helped her pack up her sketching things on the balcony and then, taking them under his arm, he followed her down to the gondola that was to take them to the Great Britain Hotel. On the journey neither said a word beyond commenting on the warmth of the day and the recent increase in mosquitos. When they arrived she took the sketching paraphernalia from him and went away up in the lift to fetch her passport, and as the elaborate iron-work of the contraption took her from his sight he found that he was holding a small handkerchief in his hand. It had evidently been caught up in the sketch-book; he would give it to her when she came down, and in the meantime he slipped it into his pocket. But he did not give it to her, and when the lift brought her back to him it remained in his pocket.

Upstairs, while Cecily had rummaged for her passport, she had wished most heartily that she could find some excuse for sending Charles Pitborough away. But the Lavenders would not be back for some hours yet, and there was nothing for it but to tie a veil more firmly over her hat and to start out with her parasol and passport for the Post Office beyond the Merceria.

Her remarks about the Admiral's gallant officers appeared to have had a softening effect on her companion, and as they left the hotel he seemed determined to be polite. When they left St Mark's Square and entered the cooler confines of a narrow paved calle between tall houses he asked her if she and Miss Lavender had visited any other ships beside the *Jupiter*.

"Oh yes. One day we had tea on a torpedo-catcher."

"And what might that be? Forgive me if my knowledge of the Royal Navy is somewhat limited."

"You are not the only one not to know what a torpedo-catcher is," she told him, happy to enlarge on the subject and keep the conversation to a safe topic. "Mrs Lavender—who came with us to chaperone us—thought it might be a net hung over the side of the ship to catch torpedoes in. It is called a gunboat, I think—a funny little craft, lying very low in the water —and the accommodation is limited in the extreme. It carries a crew of sixty or so and I cannot imagine where they all go, because the Captain's servant sleeps on top of a torpedo tube in a sort of lumber-room surrounded by luggage. The Commander's cabin is about ten foot square and only seven foot high, and it holds the fighting end of the torpedo tube as well as the usual ship's furniture. The Commander, Lieutenant Read, told us that in order to use the tube the wardroom door had to be unshipped and pieces taken out of the walls. The torpedo is then brought from amidships, suspended on a small railway from the ceiling —" She broke off, aware that he was studying her face with unaccustomed interest. "I beg your pardon. I am boring you with all this."

"Not at all. I am very interested." He wished perversely that in his more personal conversations with her he could summon up as much animation in her face.

"I thought you might be. Men are always interested in ships."

"And did you drink your tea under this—torpedo railway?"

"Oh no. We had tea in the mess." She half smiled

as she remembered the struggle they had to get Mrs
Lavender aboard, that plump lady being obstructed
by a tight skirt, high-heeled boots and the ever-present
sunshade. That they managed it at all was entirely
due to the Royal Navy. There was almost nothing,
she thought, that was beyond them. He saw the smile
and was annoyed because it had obviously been inspired by something she recollected during the afternoon in which he had had no part.

"And what was the Commander of this extraordinary ship like?" he asked, and this time he could not
quite keep the irony from his voice.

"A charming man." She was unnecessarily enthusiastic. "We met him first in your sister's house. and
he was so anxious to entertain us in his funny little
craft that we hadn't the heart to refuse him. He was
a very good dancer," she added inconsequentially.

He was about to make a second sarcastic comment
and then suppressed it and instead asked her mildly
if the Fleet's arrival had not interrupted their sight
seeing programme.

"For a tourist," he added, "your interest in Venice
seems to have been but slight during the past week.
I know Americans are always in a hurry to see everything in the shortest possible time, but usually that
is because they have a little time in which to see it,
But English people are more painstaking, their parties headed by an earnest papa like your Mr Lavender,
guide-book in hand, who carefully explains every de-
tail of every painting as you progress from one church
to another."

"There are a great number of churches in Venice,
Mr Pitborough. On our first morning we must have

looked at six, and four more and a museum in the afternoon. The pace has certainly abated somewhat since, because of the Fleet to a certain extent, but more perhaps because of the exhaustion of Mr Lavender's companions! Yesterday we did only two museums and an art gallery, and today there is the glass factory at Murano." Her face was grave again, the animation gone.

"I apologize. As tourists, I percieve you are not doing so badly." Uppermost in both minds now was the conversation he had had with her in the gondola on the night of their visit to the theatre but he did not refer to it until after they had found the Post Office and discovered a letter waiting for her there, and, as she had anticipated, it was from her mother.

"Are you not going to open it?" he asked.

"No." She knew in advance what it would contain.

"Then as it is a hot day I suggest that we go back to St Mark's Square and see what Florian's Restaurant can produce in the way of ices, and as we eat them we can perhaps return to our conversation of a week ago. There was no time to tell you about it then, but I have a solution that I think should meet your requirements—as regards the disposal of your family, when you take up your position in my house."

10

His easy assumption that he would have his way
provoked her so much that she would have liked to
leave him before he could say any more. Never, she
thought, had any woman been so teased by such a
man, but as she had no idea which of the many calles
leading off the one they were in led back to St Mark's
Square and eventually to the Great Britain Hotel, she
walked along beside him without saying a word.

He glanced at her and saw that the suggestion of
ices at Florian's was not popular, and he smiled in
spite of himself. In silence he conducted her back by
way of a street market, and here he was happy in his
choice, because the many stalls with their brightly
coloured wares, their heaped fruit and vegetables,
glittering glass necklaces and displays of lace and
leather goods drew forth her ready interest and admiration. She bought leather pencil cases for the two

boys, a leather cigar case for the General, and a white lace scarf for her mother.

"Now if I could sit here and sketch this market," she said aloud, looking down its length with pleasure, and then checked herself abruptly. "But it would be beyond my powers. You were right when you said that I need lessons. I would be quite unable to attempt so much movement of life and colour."

"In any case, you could not sit here alone and paint," he said curtly, and taking her parcels from her he went on: "I will arrange for you to have painting and drawing lessons when you are at Oatesby—also singing lessons. You have a charming voice, but it would benefit, I think, from training. Not too much— but a few lessons from a good teacher—one such as Adelina Patti for instance—would not come amiss."

Infuriating as he was, she could scarcely help smiling at his persistence. Repressing it, she said meekly: "I am sorry that you don't like my singing, Mr Pitborough."

"It is not a question of liking or disliking it," he replied gravely. "But when you entertain my guests at Oatesby I would like you to be better than you are now."

"I quite understand," she said, turning her head to smile at him with a malicious glint in her hazel eyes. "It is entirely in your own interest that you want me to have these lessons in painting and singing."

"Naturally." Once more his assurance astonished her: she did not know whether she wanted most to abuse him for it or to laugh, and again she held her tongue. They came out into the hot sunshine of St Mark's Square in silence and only when they were seated at a small table in Florian's Restaurant with ices in front of them did he say what was in his mind.

"When I first suggested that you should go through a form of marriage with me," he said, "your conditions were that you must bring your family with you to Oatesby."

"That is so," she replied firmly. "And I would add that nothing has happened to make me change my mind."

"Then perhaps what I have to suggest now may make a difference," he said. "I am willing to buy a house for your mother in Milchester, to furnish it for her and to allow her the sum of one thousand pounds a year. The house will, of course, be large enough to accommodate her and her family and the number of servants that she will need. She will be answerable to me for her accounts and what she spends, but as long as she does not overstep her income she will be free to do as she pleases."

Cecily could scarcely believe her ears, but before she could get her breath he continued calmly:

"It would be a more sensible arrangement than the one you proposed and I think upon consideration you will agree with me there. Oatesby is three miles outside the town, and although your brothers can walk in to school and back—or I might send them to boarding school—your mother would almost constantly be needing a carriage to take her into Milchester to see her friends, and I am not sure that I could always spare the extra horses. Your sister could go to her dancing classes with Janie and share her governess—though I am informed by my aunt that the lady I employ now is not very good. Apart from all this, however, I am not sure that your mother would appreciate being a permanent member of her daughter's establishment: I feel that she would prefer having her own house and servants, and at the same time the arrangement would free your uncle from the embarrassment that you say your family is to him. There is a chance, therefore, that it will meet the requirements of everybody, including myself."

As she remained speechless at this easy disposal of her and her family, he continued as if he took her assent for granted: "So we will consider the matter as decided, shall we? When would you like me to approach your uncle for his consent to the marriage? I would like to get it settled directly I get home next week, but if you would rather I waited until your return to England I am quite willing to fall in with your wishes. You will not find me an unreasonable man on the whole, I think."

"Stop!" She found her voice in a hurry. "I am sorry, Mr Pitborough, but you are going too fast and taking too much for granted. I have not said if this arrangement will be acceptable and there is my family to be considered, after all."

"Forgive me if I say that I thought I had considered them quite particularly.'

"But there is my mother's consent to be obtained before anything of the sort could be contemplated."

"Naturally. When I go to see your uncle I shall also see your mother. I don't think I have any very annoying habits," he continued thoughtfully. "I am not fussy over my food. I do not like boiled eggs and I like coffee for my breakfast, otherwise my likes and dislikes are not serious. But my housekeeper will tell you all about that, of course."

She finished her ice and put down her spoon, her eyes dark with wrath. "Has it never occurred to you to consider *my* likes and dislikes?" she demanded.

"No, but you will be perfectly free to give rein to them as and how you like."

Just for one breathless second their eyes met and she thought wildly, "He is horrible—and yet he is wonderful. He is—oh, I don't know if I hate him or if I'm half in love with him. But he is unlike any other man in the world."

Then he cut across her confused thoughts by saying coldly, "This is, after all, a business arrangement, Miss Floyd, not a personal one. In return for providing your family with a home of their own I will have a hostess for my house and a mamma for little Janie. The price you ask is high, but not more than I am prepared to pay. So what more is there to be discussed between us?"

She came to earth with a bump, the wild emotion of a minute ago stilled. "Only that I have not said yet that I am prepared to take the post you are offering me," she replied, holding her voice steady. "You take things too much for granted, Mr Pitborough, as I said just now, probably because when you first saw me you thought me to be a dowdy gawk of a girl who would suit your purpose admirably."

"You do not let me forget that, do you?" he said frowning. "Very well then, you *were* dowdy in the dreadful dress—"

"But it was difficult to make my mother's old

dresses look smart," she protested. "The dressmaker did her best."

"You mean that dress was made from one of your mother's?" He sounded incredulous.

"I have not had a new dress—one that was made for me I mean—since we left London when I was still in the schoolroom. I should have come away with Mr and Mrs Lavender with a load of my mother's old clothes in my trunk if my uncle had not put his foot down and said that I was to travel as his niece would travel, with clothes that would not shame him." She looked down at her light pretty summer dress in voile the colour of buttercups. "It had been largely my fault, I suppose: there was not enough money for us both to be well dressed, and I would not make a fuss because I was afraid of hurting my beloved uncle." She saw his eyes return to her face with a warmer expression than she had seen in them before, and re-membering the snub he had administered earlier, she flushed a little, fearing that he might think that she was asking for sympathy and understanding, or in other words dragging the whole affair on to the per-sonal plane that he so markedly disliked. She went on composedly: "This is nothing to do with you, how-ever, Mr Pitborough. I will let you have your answer before you leave next week, if you will tell me when you are going?"

"We leave on Wednesday."

"Very well. I will give you my answer on Monday. I must have time in which to consider this new propo-sition. It has raised more problems for me to solve."

"Can I not help you to solve them?" he asked in a kinder voice.

"Nobody can help me," she replied shortly. She looked at the little gold watch that had belonged to the General's mother and that she wore pinned in to the bodice of her dress. "It is time that my wanderers returned," she told him briskly. "I must go back to the hotel."

He walked back with her and as they parted at the door she took her parcels from him and then held out her hand and said frankly, "Today is Friday. You shall have your answer on Monday, Mr Pitborough. I promise you that." And then she was gone.

He took a gondola back to his sister's great house in an unusually thoughtful mood, blind to the dancing water, the sunshine on the creamy walls of the Doge's Palace, the rose red of the city's roofs, the infinite beauty of the romantic city that was Venice.

He found himself dwelling unnecessarily on the tones of Cecily's voice, on the direct look in her eyes, the warm grip of her fingers on his. The business proposition that had been intended to engage a sensible, badly dressed young woman to take his aunt's place in the household at Oatesby had suddenly become touched with unwelcome personal problems that he had not foreseen. He tried to summon up his old hatred for women and it seemed to be completely passive: he attempted to dismiss this one young woman from his mind and she would not be dismissed. Freed from the cares of her family and her selfish mother, she was assured and remarkably handsome and he thought that her eyes were the loveliest he had seen on a woman. He was more than ever determined to have her for his house, as he would have been deter-

mined to buy a painting or a piece of furniture that
had taken his fancy.

One thing he was sure of, however, was that he had
alienated her completely, and that as a result of his
clumsy handling of the situation, if she should decide
to become part of his property at Oatesby, it would
be on the terms that he had originally set down and
on no other terms at all. Oatesby was large enough to
contain them both and to separate them at the same
time irrevocably. And in his present perverse mood
he began to wonder if that was the way he really
wanted it to be.

When he got back to his sister's great house on the
Canal he found the Contessa inconveniently interested
in his afternoon with Miss Floyd. As he sat with her
in the garden, watching the small green lizards darting
about the low wall that separated it from the Grand
Canal, and fending off her curiosity, at last she asked
him outright if his visit to Venice had been in any way
connected with Cecily.

"What makes you think that?" He broke a twig
from an oleander tree behind the marble seat and began to strip the leaves from it slowly.

"The way you behave to each other when you meet
perhaps. She was almost rude to you that night at the
theatre and yet you made a point of going off with her
alone in a gondola evidently anxious to talk to her in
private. And now today you insisted on taking that
note to Lady Rand when one of my servants could
equally well have gone with it. I think you had discovered—probably through Rigby—that Miss Floyd was
to be at the Rands' this morning. He was out early, so
my maid told me. Did you send him round to the

Great Britain Hotel by any chance, Charles?" And then, as her brother did not reply: "I'm right, am I not? There is an understanding of some sort between you and Miss Floyd?"

"You were always too sharp, Miriam." He hesitated and then he told her, badly and unemotionally, the plans he had for taking Cecily into his household and the provision he intended to make for her family.

"But, Charles, you cannot do that!" She was horrified. "You do not know what Mrs Floyd is like. I have been hearing about her from Lady Rand lately, and no man in his senses would give such a woman *carte blanche* with money. Lady Rand told me that Floyd came from a well-to-do family, but that he was an uttter spendthrift, and though he had spent half his fortune before he met Louisa Masterson she quickly helped him to get through the rest, and when he died poor General Masterson had to settle a lot of their debts out of his own pocket. It that is true, Mrs Floyd could run you into many thousands of pounds."

"I think not." His smile was enigmatical. "Not many people can get the better of me in a business deal, Miriam."

She considered him thoughtfully. "No," she said then, "I do not suppose they can, in fact, I would not like to be the person who thought that he or she could. But there is another aspect to this—affair—that seems to have escaped you."

"And what is that?" He was plainly unwilling to discuss it but she went on steadily:

"I must say this and then I will say no more as I can see you are in no mood for confidences. Mamma once said to me that the Pitboroughs were too much inclined to bring business into their private lives, and that was why it was so charming to meet Wilbur Goldmeyer, who put her first from the moment he met her. You seem to have inherited the family failing, Charles. It does not seem to occur to you that Cecily Floyd is a great deal younger than you are, and that she is also a very attractive young woman. At the Admiral's ball the men were round her like bees round a honeypot. The time may come when she falls in love with another man. You do not wish, surely, to invite a second tragedy into your life?"

He moved restlessly. The oleander twig snapped in his fingers and he threw it away, his sombre eyes moving to the small craft passing on the Grand Canal beyond the garden wall, his mind on a tragic occasion in Naples some years ago.

"I think I am immune to that sort of thing now," he said at last. "It may seem to you that I am imposing a hard bargain on Cecily Floyd, but if she consents to it I can promise you that she will have complete freedom where her own friends are concerned—as long as she does not bring scandal on my name. For myself I cannot and I will not become emotionally involved with any woman again. It is for Janie that I am doing this, and for her alone. She needs somebody whose understanding and—affection—will always be there for her to turn to, apart from old Nurse Appleby: in other words she needs somebody who will take the place of her mother. It seems to me that Cecily Floyd is admirably qualified to fill the post, and that is why I offered it to her. I am hoping that she will accept."

She wanted to protest that he was still not looking

at the thing from Cecily's side of the bargain, that the time might come when, like any normal young woman, she would want a real husband, a home of her own, and children of her own instead of Janie, and that he would make it impossible for her to obtain any of these things except through the scandal of a divorce. And that this might do more damage to Janie and to them both than abandoning the whole project.

But there was something in the stiff unyielding attitude of her brother's mind that kept her silent. Gussie had a great deal to answer for: she had always to remember that.

11

At about the time that the Bishop's wife was sending out her invitations to the New Year Palace ball, an old house next door to Pitborough and Orde's bank was let for six months to a Mr Gerald Turnbull, an Australian gentleman, who let it be known almost directly he arrived in the town that he was engaged in writing a book about the sheep farmers of Australia and did not welcome visitors.

Mr William Pitborough, having called to ask him if he would like to be put up as an honorary member of the Liberal Club in Milchester—an honour that was somewhat brusquely refused—told his wife that the man was undoubtedly a rough diamond, and what was more he expressed a few doubts as to the English he would employ in writing his book. But as he had not been invited into Mr Turnbull's study to observe the pile of manuscript that was said to be there he

could not tell her what proportions the resulting book
seemed likely to take. He noticed, however, that the
house was sparsely furnished and there appeared to be
only two servants, a man and his wife who were both
on terms of great familiarity with their employer.

When Mrs William Pitborough repeated this information to Mrs Blades the Colonel's wife told her
that this was not unusual in Australia. She had a sister
married to an Australian sheep farmer and she had
heard stories of how her servants would think nothing
of going home for a week and leaving her stranded
without anybody to wait on her or cook the meals.

"While as for Christmas Day," added Mrs Blades,
"my sister always has to cook the dinner for her family
then, and for any of the hands on the farm who cannot get home."

The Colonel also called on Mr Turnbull, but when
he returned and his wife asked him his opinion of the
Australian he replied that if he was writing a book
about Australian sheep farms he knew surprisingly
little about them.

"I have met several authors in my time," he remarked, "and while I must confess I have not had a
great deal in common with them, at least they were
usually sufficiently interested in the subject on which
they were writing about to be able to talk about it.
Mr Turnbull never mentioned sheep farming in Australia once. In fact I came away with the impression
that he might be over here on an entirely different
occupation."

"But what could that be?" asked Mrs Blades.

"It would be interesting to know," said the Colonel.
Judge Kirby had much the same idea about the

newcomer when he went to call on him. "I am convinced I have seen him somewhere before," he told his wife. "His face is familiar to me. But I cannot think where it was that we met."

"Not at the Old Bailey I trust?" said Mrs Kirby, laughing.

"I should think it unlikely," said the Judge. "Although the manservant who opened the door to me was villainous enough to be at home in the dock anywhere."

It was generally agreed however that if Mr Turnbull did not wish to mix with what society Milchester could afford then he should be left to himself, and his presence among them except for a good-morning when they met in the street could be politely ignored. Which was exactly what Mr Turnbull wanted.

Pitborough and Orde's Bank had always prided itself on its happy association with its staff: the clerks who worked there were looked after well, and if any fell sick they could depend on having their positions kept open for them until they were well enough to return. Lately, moreover, Mr Charles Pitborough had instituted a fund for sickness benefit among the staff which had lifted a great deal of anxiety from the shoulders of the older members. Until then they had not dared to stay away from their work when they were ill because they would lose their pay. This was not to say that the bank encouraged malingerers and the bank doctor would always visit any man who was away from his place in the office for more than a day or two to discover if the illness was real, or simply an excuse to have a day off for the Milchester races.

Among Pitborough and Orde's half-dozen clerks

there was a rather unhappy little man by the name of Harold Pretty, married to an empty-headed wife who was habitually discontented with her lot. Nearly every evening when he returned home she would complain that she would like to have certain things for herself and the house, which he would explain to her as patiently as he could that it was not possible for her to have.

One night that April over their evening meal when she had been particularly unreasonable he had reminded her sharply that his salary was now the highest that he could expect and they would have to manage on it. "Others with families of children are living comfortably on less than we have, my dear," he added. The Prettys had no family.

"You have been with Pitborough's for sixteen years," she said, her voice rising. "It is time you had a higher salary. It isn't fair."

"I started as we all start at Pitborough's with ninety pound a year, which was increased every year until now it has risen to three hundred pound. I cannot expect more than that."

"I am sure bigger banks would pay you more," she complained.

"If you mean the joint-stock banks then I daresay they might pay more in the end but I am too old now to move. My starting salary with another bank would be a pittance to what I am earning now."

"They've worked you hard enough all these years," she said peevishly. "You ought to be head clerk by now instead of that doddering old Summerscales."

"Sam Summerscales has been with the bank for nearly forty years." Poor Mr Pretty prayed for patience. "He knows as much—and more—than some of the partners. Mr Charles would sooner cut off his right hand than replace old Sam: there's years of work in him yet."

"What is his salary?" asked Mrs Pretty resentfully. "Four hundred pound a year?"

"As I don't ask to see the wages lists," said Mr Pretty righteously, "I can't tell you."

"Then you should ask to see them. No wonder Mrs Summerscales can have new curtains for her parlour. Mine can fall to bits and nobody cares." She began to cry. "I hate Pitborough's—I hate Milchester—with all the fine ladies driving out in their carriages and looking down on the likes of us. I hate them and I wish I were dead!" And she ran out of the room into the parlour and pulled her shabby curtains there with such viciousness that the hem of one of them was nearly torn off, which made her cry harder than ever.

Mr Pretty left his supper unfinished and went out of the house, slamming the front door behind him. He knew he ought not to have said what he did about the other clerks and their families: it was always a sore point with Polly that she had never had a child. But sometimes he felt that she was a most unreasonable woman, and he supposed gloomily that all women were the same. But when he saw some of his fellow clerks out on a Sunday they did not seem to be unduly depressed, in fact they were remarkably cheerful, and their children were well kept and their wives nicely dressed, although some of them had less than he had to live on.

The April evening was soft with rain, and he turned up the collar of his coat and went into a bar of the

Tilverton Arms for a pint of beer. He felt that he needed it. As he sat there a man with the face of a prize fighter and cauliflower ears came and sat down at the little marble-topped table beside him and gave him good evening.

"If it *is* a good evening," said Mr Pretty lugubriously.

"You want to come out to Australia mate," said the man with the cauliflower ears. "Your wife and kids would love it down under."

"Haven't got any kids," said Mr Pretty in a depressed voice.

"Then your wife maybe."

"Oh *she* would like it," said Mr Pretty bitterly. "It's anything for a change where she is concerned. She would like any country that would take her away from Milchester."

"I can't say as I blame her for that. Milchester is a dead and alive sort of hole, and I bet you aren't earning enough to keep a fly alive."

Mr Pretty did not think his earnings were the concern of a stranger and drank his beer in offended silence. The man continued after a moment:

"Of course in Queensland we pay a man real wages, not the sort that pass for them over here. If it isn't a rude question, may I ask where you are working, sir?"

"At Pitborough and Orde's Bank," said Mr Pretty briefly.

"Indeed?" said the stranger as if this were news to him. "Now in Australia a man with years of banking experience can ask a thousand a year and get it. We are short of people with brains there and we know how to keep 'em."

Again Mr Pretty held his peace but he drank his beer more thoughtfully and did not refuse when the stranger asked if he would like some more. By the time they parted the gentleman had found out quite a lot about Mr and Mrs Pretty, and about the bank, while Mr Pretty had found out very little about the man with the cauliflower ears except that his name was Ed Sorrel and that he worked for Mr Turnbull at Kingsdown House next door to the bank. When they parted he said casually, "If you ever think of emigrating to Australia, mate, come and see Mr Turnbull one evening. He'll tell you more than I can about the opportunities out there for gentlemen like yourself."

When Mr Pretty got home he was forgiving to his wife, because after all she had a lot to try her and he ought not to have said anything about the clerks who had families of children, and as they got into bed that night he asked her if she would like to emigrate.

"Where to?" she asked.

"Australia. Lovely climate out there, so I'm told— hot for most of the year—and the salary I'd earn in a bank in Sydney, doing what I'm doing now, would be a thousand a year."

"Ooh!" Her eyes sparkled. "How do you set about looking for such a post?"

"I think the first thing I ought to do would be to go and see Mr Turnbull."

"And who is Mr Turnbull?"

"The Australian gentleman who's taken Kingsdown House, next to the bank."

"Oh, *him!*" said Mrs Pretty.

"Yes, him," said Mr Pretty. "I believe he could be quite a lot of use to yours truly."

"Well," said Mrs Pretty, "if you ask me it's time somebody was a bit of use to you, Harold Pretty."

Ed Sorrel happened to be in the Tilverton Arms on the following night, and when Mr Pretty approached him rather diffidently, asking if he could arrange an appointment for him with Mr Turnbull, he told him to drink up and come along right away.

"He may be in London tomorrow," he told him. "Or in Scotland. Or even in Paris. A real live wire is Mr Turnbull. But I know he is there tonight."

Mr Pretty went with him feeling rather apprehensive, but Mr Turnbull immediately made him feel at home by offering him a brandy and hot water, and making him sit down by the fire on that chilly evening, because the warm rain of the night before had changed to outbreaks of hail, in the way of an English April.

They talked about Australia, and although Mr Turnbull did not know of a Sydney bank that was craving at that precise moment for an English clerk, he said he would write off at once to a banking friend there and see what they had to offer.

"As far as I am concerned I like Milchester," he said. "And I am very much inclined to settle here for a time. Mind you, I am a rich man, which means that I can afford to move whenever the mood takes me. But I would like a permanent home in England, as well as my house in Sydney, which is very large indeed. It would make Kingsdown House look like a cottage. In fact," he added, "I have a butler and twelve servants as I do a great deal of entertaining out there.

The price that is being asked for Kingsdown House is not a high one by Australian standards, but I think somebody else is after it, and I am pretty sure that the somebody concerned is the bank next door."

"The bank?" Mr Pretty was surprised. "Do you mean Pitborough and Orde's, sir?"

"Yes. Have you heard nothing about it?"

"Nothing. Not that it is likely that they would confide in me," added Mr Pretty bitterly.

"Well, I have heard they are the interested parties, but I shall be obliged if you keep this strictly between ourselves. It may be an unfounded rumour: you know how gossip spreads in a town like Milchester. You will know though how easy—or how difficult—it may be for the bank building to be merged with Kingsdown House, and I'd be glad of your opinion, Mr Pretty, on the matter." And then, while Mr Pretty sat silent turning it over in his mind, he opened a drawer in a desk and took from it a rolled-up plan of a house. "Look," he said, "Have a glance at this—it is the plan of Kingsdown House. Tell me what is on the other side of the party wall—is it a room or a corridor or the clerks' office, or what?"

Mr Pretty spread the plan out in front of him and studied it carefully. "Why," he said then, "the partners' rooms are the other side of the wall here, Mr Turnbull. The corridor that leads to them must end t'other side of where you've got your bookcase. If they did buy this house there would be no trouble there: it would simply be a matter of knocking a doorway through there, and probably moving the partners' rooms into this house. Wait though!" He checked himself with a comical expression of dismay. "It might not be so easy after all! The wall dividing the two houses is at least three to four foot thick. They found that out when they were doing some alterations to the cellars—vaults, as we call them."

"Three to four foot thick," echoed Mr Turnbull thoughtfully. "These English houses are certainly built to last! And the vaults, as you call them—what do they use them for?"

"Oh, all the deed-boxes containing important documents or papers belonging to our customers are stored down there—things like the deeds of properties and wills and so on. And then, of course, there is the safe—more like a strong-room really, with thick steel sides and door."

"I'll bet they don't trust you clerks with the key to that!"

"Gracious no. The partners have sets of keys—to the vaults and the safe you know. And, of course, Mr Summerscales has a set, but that is all. Mr Charles Pitborough is always saying that he'd like to see the strong-room more secure: he'd like to have the steel walls strengthened and two steel doors instead of one, but Mr Orde—he's the Senior Partner when he troubles himself to visit the bank, but he mostly lives in Lancashire—he says it was secure enough for Mr Charles's father and it is secure enough for him. There are very strong bars over the windows down there, of course, and with the one door to the vaults locked, I daresay he is right and it is safe enough."

"And I daresay there is a night watchman," added Mr Turnbull.

"Oh no, we don't have anything like that!" Mr Pretty was amused at the idea. "They may have 'em in your banks in Sydney, and they may have 'em in London banks —I can't say about that. But for a bank like Pitborough and Orde's in a sleepy town like Milchester there's no need for night watchmen and such. We have a day porter of course, but he's more to run errands than anything else. A sort of bank messenger, if you take my meaning."

Mr Turnbull took his meaning even more fully than he realized.

"Mind you," went on Mr Pretty, becoming more talkative every minute under the comforting brandy. "Mr Pitborough is as good as a night watchman any day. He is often here at night himself, working long after everybody has gone home, and he'd know at once if there was anybody about. Nobody knows when he will be here, you see, and he's a very sharp gentleman, is Mr. Charles."

"He sounds it indeed. Well, thank you very much Mr Pretty. My man said you were clever, but I did not anticipate that you would have such a complete grasp of things." He poured more brandy into his visitor's glass. "I will certainly write to my friend in Sydney, but if I were you I would not mention our conversation to anybody at the bank. If they discover that you are looking for a better post you may find yourself dismissed without a reference, if I know anything about English employers."

Mr Pretty wanted to say that in fairness to Mr Charles, Pitborough and Orde's was not like that at all, and the partners would never stand in the way of one of their clerks if he had a chance to better himself, but the brandy made him feel slightly confused and also rather indignant with Pitborough and Orde's, though he did not quite know why. He allowed Ed to help him into his coat and muffler and show him to the door.

As he walked home in the darkness and the cold air cleared his head Mr Pretty wished they had had more time to discuss Australia; the sort of house he could expect to have there for example, and the way people lived, and so on. But no doubt when he had heard from his friend in Australia Mr Turnbull would send for him—he had taken his home address—and they would have another discussion before he made up his mind to go.

But a salary of a thousand a year did not leave room for much doubt in Mr Pretty's mind. On that sum he could live like a gentleman and keep a carriage, and his wife could curtain her house from attic to cellar.

12

As the days went by, Harold Pretty found that far from losing interest in him, Mr Turnbull's friendship became flatteringly warmer every time they met, while on his side he developed the habit of dropping in to the Tilverton Arms on his way home of an evening to see if Ed happened to be there. More often than not he was there, and when this occurred, after a drink or two he would invite him back with him again to Kingsdown House where Mr Turnbull would be ready with his excellent brandy to talk about Australia and the good things that awaited people who were wise enough to emigrate to that idyllic country.

When Polly protested at being left so much on her own the stories he had to tell her when he came home more than compensated her for her lonely evenings, and on one occasion Mr Turnbull invited her with Harold to dinner at Kingsdown House. And although she wished he did not smell quite so strong of brandy, she was impressed by his stories of his house in Sydney and the numbers of servants he had there to wait on him and his friends, while his politeness to herself, and the compliments he paid Harold on having such a pretty wife placed him at once in her mind as a real gentleman. She was more impressed still when he sent them home in a cab, as a lady and her husband should be sent, and she hoped that Mr Charles Pitborough was working late that night, so that he would be able to see them going home like gentry after their evening with his neighbour.

During these visits Harold Pretty did not learn quite as much about Australia as Mr Turnbull learned about Pitborough and Orde's Bank. He learned for instance that the high wall topped with spikes that separated the neglected garden of Kingdown House from the courtyard of the bank premises had a drop of at least fifteen feet on the other side. This was a good thing, because it shielded Ed from observation when he dug the border under the wall on the Kingsdown House side, increasing its height with loads of black earth mixed with rubble that to anyone with a suspicious turn of mind might have seemed to be taken from beneath a cellar. It was a pity, Mr Turnbull felt, that Mr Charles Pitborough appeared to have such a strong interest in the bank that he could not be depended upon to go home at the end of the day as any nomal gentleman should. It was quite unnecessary for a man in that position to be such a glutton for work: it showed either an unhealthy state of mind or a nasty, nosy disposition.

And then one evening, while Mr Pretty sat drinking

Mr Turnbull's brandy, he let out that Mr Charles Pitborough had astonished his partners and his employees by taking a holiday abroad. And when Mr Turnbull asked who was taking charge in his absence Mr Pretty laughed and said that Mr William Pitborough would be there, but one could scarcely say that he would be in charge of anything.

"Doesn't he like work then?" asked Mr Turnbull.

"That he doesn't. He's a bit of a gay dog," said Harold knowingly.

"Not like Mr Charles then?"

"M'dear feller," said Mr Pretty, slurring his words slightly, "He's no more like Mr Charles than I'm like tha' bo'l of brandy."

Adroitly Mr Turnbull poured him another glass. "No working late with him, then?" he observed genially.

Mr Pretty laughed. "Why, he don't get into th' bank till 'leven in th' mornings," he said. "An' he's off again at one for his dinner—luncheon, as Mrs William calls it. Fine lady, is Mrs William. Then he's not back from that till three, and he's off again home puncshul —punc'shly—at five or sometimes four, if the mood takes him till 'leven next morning."

Mr Turnbull said Mr William was a wise man. "In Australia," he told him, "a bank like Pitborough's might not open at all on a Saturday. Is Mr William there on a Saturday, Mr Pretty?"

Mr Pretty suppressed a hiccup and said very seldom, in a melancholy tone. "He leaves everything to Mr Summerscales if he wants to go out with his wife that day," he added.

"Now that's what I call good business," said Mr

Turnbull approvingly, "Why keep a dog and bark yourself?"

" 'Cept when you're the dog," said Mr Pretty bitterly. "I get a bit tired of doing all the barking, Mr Turnbull."

"Well, you won't have to do it much longer," Mr Turnbull assured him cheerfully, and sent Ed with him to see him safely home.

On the last Friday night before Charles was due to return William's conscience, coupled with a large, rich dinner at the Liberal Club, gave him a restless night, reminding him that Charles would want a meticulous account of the hours put in at the bank in his absence. And if he had not put in sufficient for what his cousin regarded as being essential he might be in for some uncomfortable moments. There were times when Mr Charles Pitborough's tongue could be very scathing indeed.

On Saturday morning, therefore, he turned up in his room at the bank at eleven o'clock, throwing the clerks and old Summerscales into utter confusion, as nobody had expected him in at all that day. What was more, he went through the accounts for the entire time that his cousin had been away, and it needed a great deal of extra work on the part of Mr Summerscales to explain them to him. The old man did not grudge the time thus given however: like his employers, he had the prosperity of the bank at heart.

William's interest in the bank's affairs lasted until three o'clock, when he took his hat from its peg and drawing on his gloves declared that he had done enough until Monday morning. He glanced out of the window as he spoke and over the wire blind he

was horrified to observe an antiquated carriage drawing up outside Pitborough and Orde's, and a claw-like
hand beckoning from the window. He saw Summerscales hurry out, and from his equally rapid return
William guessed he had been sent to summon one of
the partners.

"Oh God," groaned William, watching this panto-
mime. "Sir Matthew Billing back again! Why the devil
couldn't he have waited until Charles was back?"

Sir Matthew was one of the bank's wealthiest customers, in fact even Joseph Orde said that he did not
know how much he was worth. He owned a dilapidated house and a large, neglected estate in the country, but he lived mostly abroad, and on the rare occasions when he returned to England he usually brought
with him some problem concerning investments for
Charles to solve, and as a rule such problems involved
a great deal of money.

Today, however, it seemed that investments were
not in question, and Mr Turnbull, watching from the
window of the house next door, saw that the hand
that summoned Mr William Pitborough to wait on the
occupant of the carriage belonged to a very old gentleman, rather like a tortoise in appearance, who was
warmly wrapped up on that June afternoon in over-
coat, plaid rug, muffler and deer-stalker hat. It appeared to the watcher that the only reason for his
visit was to deliver an untidily done-up brown paper
parcel that was lying beside him on the carriage seat
into the hands of the junior partner of the bank.

When Mr Pretty met Ed in the Tilverton Arms that
evening he was more pressing than usual that he
should come and see Mr Turnbull later on, and as

they sat round the fire with their brandy and water in the chilly dining-room of Kingsdown House Mr Turnbull asked what had been in the parcel that he had seen delivered to the bank that afternoon. "Does that old gentleman leave some of his clothing there to be put in your vaults?" he asked.

Harold Pretty laughed. "Oh," he said, "that was Sir Matthew Billing, a very peculiar old gentleman. Mr Summerscales says he's a real eccentric, but I'd call him cracked. You may not believe this, but in strict confidence that parcel contained two hundred thousand pounds in bearer bonds. He collects them on his travels abroad and every few years he comes home with a bundle of 'em for the bank to keep for him."

"Two hundred thousand pounds!" exclaimed Mr Turnbull. "And in bearer bonds, did you say?"

"Lucky thing Mr Charles is still away," chuckled Mr Pretty. "If he'd been there this afternoon he'd have had us all checking and listing and cutting the coupons from those bonds before he put 'em away himself in the safe. But not Mr William! He soon stopped Mr Summerscales when he suggested he should tell us all to stay on and help him to check 'em. "They've travelled across Europe in a brown paper parcel," says Mr William, grinning all over his face. "So it won't hurt if we keep 'em in that same parcel in our safe until Monday. I'm not opening up the bank on Sunday just for old Billing," says he. So he sealed the parcel all over with the bank's seal and Mr Summerscales and me took it down to the vaults."

"Oh, so you went with him, did you?" said Mr Turnbull.

"Why yes, Mr Summerscales always insists that one of us goes with him when he has to open the safe. It's a rule of the bank."

"So the two of you just put the parcel in the safe and left it there until Monday? Are there many more parcels like that in the bank's safe, Mr Pretty?"

"Oh no!" Harold Pretty laughed contemptuously. "The safe is kept for money and bank notes chiefly— the partners reckon to keep about fifteen thousand pounds there all told, in case of emergencies. And then there are items of valuable jewellery belonging to some of our customers, but most of them have safes and strong-rooms in their houses and don't trouble us with that sort of thing. And I tell you, Mr Turnbull, when I see those leather bags of sovereigns on the shelves, each of them containing five hundred pound, and I have to work a year for nearly half of that, I wonder why I stay on at Pitborough's." He paused, looking at his Australian friend wistfully, "You can't have heard from Sydney yet I know," he said, "but I daresay you will have a letter soon?"

"I am expecting a telegram at almost any time now," said Mr Turnbull cheerfully. "My banker friend will have received my letter by this time and I told him to telegraph when he has found the best post he can for you. I said the salary was to be at least a thousand a year, because you are worth that amount of money to any employer. I gave him your address, and I think that when he has found what you want he will probably telegraph you direct to come out on the next boat. And at the same time he will telegraph to the bank to credit you with the money that is needed to get you and your wife out there."

Mr Pretty went off home, his head filled with dizzy dreams of prosperity in Australia, where he would be recognized by everyone as somebody, and if at the same time he felt some slight apprehension as to what Mr Charles Pitborough might have to say about the activities he had been indulging in behind his back, he soon dismissed it from his mind. The young clerks were always warned when they took up posts there not to discuss any of the bank's business with anybody outside, but he had been there for sixteen years. He knew by this time whom he could trust, and when to open his mouth and when to keep it shut.

After the housekeeper had shown him out—Ed had disappeared early in the evening—Mr Turnbull beckoned the woman back into the room and asked in a low voice how her husband was getting on.

"He must be through by now," he said.

"He should be. There was only another foot to go last night, but it's the shoring up that's the hard work. He reckons he'll come out the other side of the party wall near the window. That party wall is four foot thick, Pretty did not tell a lie." She added: "I only hope it'ull be worth it, Jake Turnbull."

"There's a parcel in that safe worth more than our wildest dreams," he said grinning. "So long as he can get into it."

"He's had harder things to crack than bank safes." Mrs Ed was contemptuous. Had there not been a jeweller's in Paris, and that gold bullion haul in Berlin, both safes in question said to be unbreakable?

Mr Turnbull nodded, reassured. "We've got until Sunday night," he told her. "Not a moment longer. When he's ready I'll join him—and by the way have you got the sacks ready to put over the windows of the vaults next door before we light the lantern?"

"They're piled up in the cellar waiting. You don't think they will be seen from the outside?"

"No. Those windows, according to our Mr Pretty, look out onto the yard at the back, and on a Sunday the gates to the yard are locked and bolted from the inside. If we lighted a lantern down there though without the sacks obscuring the windows there might be some nosy individuals who would remember that Charles Pitborough is abroad and would want to know what was going on. You can't be too careful."

It was at that moment that Ed returned. He looked extremely dirty and the knees of his trousers were caked with earth. "I'm through," he said triumphantly. "And I've looked at the safe. It's not one that I've met before, mind, and I think it's of solid steel. It 'ull take all of twelve hours to get the door open."

Then you'd better have something to eat and go back to it," Mr Turnbull said. "As long as you can do it, that is."

"Oh yes. I can do it."

"Then we'll start packing. But put the sacks up first whatever you do. There's two hundred thousand pounds there, waiting for us, and we don't want to risk anything now, do we?"

Early on Sunday morning a cab was summoned to Kingsdown House to take Mr Turnbull to the railway station to catch the eight o'clock train to London.

Ed went with him, carrying a valise in the bottom of which was a brown-paper parcel, sealed with Pitborough and Orde's seal, the motto of which was, rather misleadingly, "What I have I hold."

During the evening Mrs Ed emerged from the house with a quantity of luggage: she told the cabby that she had been sent for by her sister in Newcastle who had suddenly been taken ill.

*   *   *   *   *

When she got back to the Great Britain Hotel that Friday afternoon Cecily had opened her mother's letter and was surprised to discover that she wrote from a friend's house in Cheltenham, where she was staying for a change of air.

The fact was that the letters that Cecily had written to her family so assiduously had the opposite effect on Mrs Floyd from what their writer had intended, and only served to increase her resentment and sense of injury.

The interest and accounts of the scenery and her amusing little anecdotes about their fellow guests in the hotels where they stayed made her feel quite ill with envy, and her complaints became so manifold and her temper so sharp that her family and her brother, not to mention the General's servants, had been utterly relieved when she decided to visit her old friend Julia Merton in Cheltenham. None of her children considered her in the least, she told Mrs Merton as she wrote imploring her to save her from a nervous breakdown. She had always done her best for them all, but her daughter Cecily had recently gone off with rich friends quite heartlessly, with a number of new dresses, knowing how much her mother would have to sacrifice to buy them for her.

I'm afraid, she ended up, *it will only be after I am gone that my children will learn what an unselfish mother they had.*

None of this was mentioned in her letter to Cecily. Dear Julia had invited her to spend some weeks with her, she said, and she had gladly accepted. The exertions in the house in Milchester had been too much for her and she was thankful to have a rest.

13

In Venice it was hotter than ever during the next few days and on the Monday morning, as it was nearing the end of her brother's visit, Miriam suggested that she should hire a boat and take Charles and Janie and Nurse Appleby with her own brood and their nurse, to the island of Lido for a day by the seashore.

"The Adriatic coast will be so refreshing after this heat," she told her brother enthusiastically. "We will take a picnic and Janie can paddle in the sea with her cousins, and they can build sand-castles, and Mr Tilverton shall come with us, and Miss Lavender and Miss Floyd and Miss Lavender's parents if such an expedition would appeal to them. The servants can follow in another boat with the picnic baskets and the wine. Unless, of course, you would not like Miss Floyd and her friends to be of the party?" She paused, waiting for his answer, as he did not seem to share her enthusiasm for it.

- "My dear girl, invite whom you please," he said. "But if you are going to fill your boats with children and young ladies and provisions I think Tilverton and I will take the steamboat out to the island, which will take ten minutes as against your three quarters of an hour. We will then be able to indulge in sea-baths there before your arrival."

And although she abused him for shirking his part in the picnic, she sent an invitation to the Great Britain Hotel and was not unduly disappointed when the girls alone accepted it.

Mrs Lavender happened to be laid low with a sick headache that morning, caused, she thought, by the humidity of the weather, and Mr Lavender said that he would stay with her. He was anxious to save his stomach from the rigours of Italian picnic food. Ordinary Italian food was bad enough, but the thought of what might be provided for a picnic sent shudders down his spine.

Punctually at half past ten a large craft called up at the steps opposite the hotel and the girls came down to be received gaily by the Contessa and her party, the two nurses doing their best to control the children's high spirits and prevent them from falling into the water.

Miriam explained that her brother and his friend were anxious to take advantage of the salt-water baths on the island, but added that they intended to join them for luncheon. "And in the meantime we will be able to stroll on the sands and look for the beautiful sea-shells there. You girls must collect some to take home."

The girls had brought parasols and thin scarves with them to keep some of the fierceness of the sun's rays from their shoulders, and as they moved out into the lagoon they were glad of it, because even the breeze was warm. Five gondoliers rowed with a will, not in the least deterred by the heat of the morning, and they were followed by five more in the second boat where servants guarded the hampers of provisions.

On the journey to the island Cecily was glad of the men's absence, as the children's chatter and the Contessa's gay nonsense made her forget for a time the problem that had overshadowed the morning ever since she woke. She had spent half the night thinking about the reply that she must give Charles Pitborough before the day was out, and she still found it hard to find an answer.

If she consented to the scheme he had put forward for her mother, then her uncle would be free from them all, and her mother would have her own house in Milchester. But would Mrs Floyd keep within the income that was proposed for her use? Would she not still apply to her brother for assistance if she ran through Charles Pitborough's allowance and dare not ask for more? Cecily felt that she could not say to him outright, "My mother is so extravagant that if you offer her a thousand a year she will spend two, and if you offer her two thousand she will spend three. She has no idea of economy at all."

Because if she said as much in trying to be fair to him, she might be accused of unfairness to her mother. It had not been easy for Mrs Floyd to accept the few

hundreds a year that was all that her brother could
save for her after everything was paid, when she had
been accustomed to ordering what she liked and never
seeing the bills.

In the meantime she was glad to see that Rosalind
seemed to have regained some of her gaiety that had
been hers when the Fleet was in port. Ever since that
first day in Venice until the sailors came to distract
her thoughts, she had been remarkably quiet and sub-
dued, and when Cecily had tackled her with it the
night before she had admitted that the cause of it all
was Mr Tilverton's changed attitude towards herself.

"It is a dreadful thing," she said mournfully, "when
you are in love with a man who cares nothing for you.
In these last weeks, Cis, I have come nearer to understanding how poor Mr Ferndean must have felt than
I ever have before."

"Mr Ferndean?" Cecily did not understand. "Have
you heard from him since we have been here then?"

"No, it is nothing to do with him." Rosalind winked
back tears. "It is Barnaby—Mr Tilverton, I mean.
When he said goodbye in the lane outside Mrs Chadwell's cottage I was certain that he loved me as much
as I loved him. And when we met again so unexpectedly in Lady Rand's drawing-room here I felt that
he was as delighted to see me again as I was to see
him. I saw nobody but him that evening, and he
seemed to have no interest in anybody but me. And
then, the next morning, he was quite changed—so cold
and distant. I am convinced that his friend, Mr Pitborough, must have said something to him. Maybe he
thinks I am not good enough to marry a Tilverton!
I know Barnaby—that is, Mr Tilverton—has a tre-

mendous opinion of Charles Pitborough and I dare
say he would be swayed by anything he said."

"But I don't think Mr Pitborough would interfere
in anything like that." Cecily felt bound to defend
her prospective employer, though she did not know
why she should go to such trouble on his behalf.

"Then why has Barnaby changed so much since
that first day?" demanded Rosalind. "Since they have
been back from Chioggia I have seen him looking at
me so sadly sometimes as if he really does love me—
but something has come between us, and he cannot
do anything to surmount it. I am convinced that
somebody has said something—done something—to
show him that it is no use for him to think of me any
more, and if it wasn't Mr Pitborough then I wish I
knew who it was who said it, and what it was that
they said."

Cecily could not help her except to suggest that
there might be a girl at home that Lord Tilverton
wished him to marry.

"Lord Tilverton washed his hands of him years
ago," Rosalind told her and there the matter rested.

In the boat this morning however Rosalind appeared
to have regained her old spirits. Her face glowed with
the salt breeze that met them, her eyes caught some of
the sparkle from the dancing sea, and her laughter
joined that of the children's. The island being reached
the two gentlemen were there to meet them, refreshed
after their salt-water baths, and waiting with convey-
ances drawn by straw-hatted horses to take the party
and its picnic to the shore on the far side.

The Contessa said that she was sure the girls must
be as cramped as she was herself, and they would all

prefer to walk, and they set out with the two men, leaving the children and nurses and picnic baskets to follow them in the carriages.

As they left the square and shops and reached the pleasant tree-lined road that led to the colder air that blew from the Adriatic the Contessa took her brother's arm with Cecily on her other side, while Rosalind and Barnaby walked behind them.

As they walked the distance between the couple and the three lengthened considerably, and in fact they seemed to be in no hurry to catch them up, Rosalind's hand being in the young man's arm and both of them engaged in earnest conversation. Glancing back from time to time Cecily hoped that they were finding an explanation for the coolness that had spoiled her friend's stay in Venice, and when they arrived at the spreading sands she saw with pleasure that it was so. Happiness lighted the two young faces in a way that was unmistakable, and after the children had arrived and were paddling under the stern eyes of their nurses Rosalind joined Cecily in her search for sea-shells and under the pretext of looking for them too told her all about it.

"He started by saying that he supposed when I got home I should be making preparations for my wedding," she said. "And when I asked what wedding, he said why, to Mr Ferndean, and he was astonished when I said I was not going to marry him. And do you know, Cis, it was Mamma who told him that I was— naughty Mamma to tell such a fib! But it doesn't matter, not now." She stopped and picked up a handful of shells and sorting them through the palm of her hand. "Now that we know we love each other, Mamma can tell what fibs she likes. She will never make me marry Mr Ferndean, and neither will Papa." She tossed back the shells on the sand and laughed. "We are going to do nothing deceitful or underhand. This evening when we return to the hotel Barnaby is going to see Papa at once and ask his consent to our becoming engaged."

"But do you think he will give it, Ros?"

"I do not think he will for one moment," admitted Rosalind frankly. "But that will not matter. I shall consider myself to be engaged to Barnaby, and by the time that I am twenty-one maybe he will be in a position to marry, or Papa may have relented. *Something* will have happened to let us marry." she added ecstatically, "I am convinced of that. Because no two people could love each other as we do and fail to marry in the end."

Cecily said she hoped that it would be so and wished them every happiness, and she found herself faintly envious because of the confidence they had in each other and in the future. As Rosalind ran off to join Barnaby and Charles and his sister in selecting a spot for their picnic she compared their lot with hers, and found no pleasure in it at all. She brushed the sand from the few shells she had collected and followed Rosalind more slowly to where the picnic cloths were being set out in the lee of a line of scrubby trees growing down by the shore. The little girls' skirts were untucked from their drawers, the little boy's trousers were unrolled, and soon the party settled down to do justice to the food with hearty appetites.

The Contessa teased her brother into a smile or

two, young Tilverton's spirits were as high as the sky, and Cecily asked grave questions about the defences of the island and when they were built. The nurses were entirely occupied in keeping insects out of the cold pies and sand out of the barley water that had been brought for the refreshment of their charges.

It was not until they had finished the meal, even Janie declaring that she could eat no more, that the Contessa remarked that the sun had gone in. "Would you believe," she said with a slight shiver, "that so warm a day could suddenly go so grey and cold?"

Charles gave a quick look at the sky, where black clouds were beginning to muster from across the sea, and said it looked as if a storm were brewing, and almost as he said it the first flash of lightning rent the heavens, followed immediately by a great clap of thunder.

The servants hastily appeared from beyond the trees and began to repack the hampers at speed, and at the same time heavy drops began to fall, threatening an imminent deluge.

They looked about and saw a couple of ruined stone huts not far away. "We'll make for those," Charles told his sister. "You take your boy, I'll take the girls and Nurse will follow with Janie."

The nurses, however, were busy collecting the children's possessions and it was Cecily who took Janie's hand and ran with her to the larger of the two huts, while Barnaby slipped his arm round Rosalind's waist and hurried her towards the smaller one.

"Isn't this fun?" said Janie as they ran. "When there is a storm at home Nurse covers the mirror in the night nursery with a towel, and draws all the curtains. I think she's frightened of storms. I'm not. I love them. Are you frightened of storms, Miss Floyd?"

"I am not."

"I thought you weren't. I shouldn't think you are afraid of anything, are you?"

"Why do you think that?"

The little girl's hand tightened on hers. "Because you look like a brave sort of person."

They had arrived at the hut by this time and Charles Pitborough, having heard the last part of this conversation waited to see what Cecily would say. It annoyed him that the smile that never appeared for him now favoured his daughter as Cecily met Pudding's enquiring eyes. "The important thing," she told her, "is to look brave, even if you are shaking in your shoes."

The nurses arrived, but nobody seemed to know what had happened to the servants with the hampers and there was no time to find out because as they arrived the deluge started.

The sagging roof did little to hold out the rain: it poured through the holes in it and Cecily's silk parasol did little to keep it out. It began to run down the walls and Charles borrowed one of the children's wooden spades to make a channel for it, in which the children delightedly joined him. As he worked with them Cecily watched his usually cold face warm with rare humour as he teased them and laughed with them, keeping their attention off the lightning and thunder outside, and she wondered what had gone wrong in the life of this austere man to make him so gentle and understanding with children and so unyielding and hateful with adults.

If only it had been different, she thought: if only the proposition that he had made to her had been inspired by a love equal to that of the young people in the hut next door! However much he had been hurt in the past it was unforgivable that he had made such a proposition to her, but as she watched him with the children she knew she was going to accept it, if only for the sake of Janie.

The rain began to lift and it was suggested that they should make for the landing stage without delay. The carrozzas had gone with the horses in case the storm should make them bolt.

"I suggest that we catch the next steamboat," Charles said. "It is no good starting out for a three-quarter-of-an-hour trip in an open boat, Miriam my dear. Those black clouds over the sea look as if we may not have seen the last of the storm yet. The servants can follow in the boats later."

Young Tilverton emerged from the smaller hut with a smiling Rosalind beside him and volunteered to take the Contessa's youngest, the boy, on his shoulders, while Charles said he would take Janie pickaback. Nurse Appleby here had something to say, however. She had somehow mislaid the coat she had brought for Miss Janie: she thought she must have left it in the boat, she had been so beset at the time they came ashore. It would be better for her to run with her cousins: that way they would all keep warm.

Certainly the temperature had dropped, and suddenly the air was much colder. Cecily saw the disappointment in Janie's face and taking the light scarf she had brought with her she hastily wrapped it round her. "There," she said gently, "that will keep you warm."

"She is too heavy to carry far anyway," said Charles abruptly. He gave his daughter a little push forward. "Give Miss Floyd back her scarf and run with your cousins as Nurse told you."

Janie was quite willing to run, but not to part with the scarf. She pulled it tightly round her, gave them an impish grin, and ran off as fast as her legs would carry her.

"I beg 'your pardon." Her father was obviously annoyed with her. "I'm afraid she has not yet learned to be obedient. I will fetch your scarf: you will need it to keep off the drips from the trees."

"Please let Janie keep it." Cecily put up her ruined parasol. "This is no longer beautiful but at least it will serve me as well." And she joined the rest of the party as they set off for the jetty.

Here they were fortunate in finding a steamer just coming in and the nurses and children were stowed away in the cabin with the ladies, the men staying to see that they were not too much jostled by an influx of tourists who had also been caught in the storm.

As she watched Charles with Janie, Cecily found that the moment at Florian's when she felt she might be in love with him was back with her again. His mouth was no longer taut, his eyes were as tender as any man's could be, and though it was all for Janie she knew that she would go to Oatesby when the time came, though they lived as far apart as the poles in the great house, only meeting once or twice a day at meals. Because if they lived in the same house she must be careful to see that they did not meet more often, in case she might inadvertently show him one day that the attraction he had for her was deeper than any she had ever known. And that would never do: she could see in advance the curl of his lip, the look in his eye, summing her up and finding her wanting in the common sense that had inspired him to invite her to be an inmate of his house.

The boat started, with black clouds of smoke, and the small cabin was crowded to suffocation. Murmuring an excuse she slipped outside the shelter of the deserted deck at the stern of the vessel. Here she was transfixed by the sky, a brilliant blue beneath the clouds as if somebody was rolling up a carpet and putting it away. And beneath it, on the horizon, like the setting of a stage, the shining line of the Italian Alps. It was a phenomenon she remembered having read about in Mr Lavender's guide-book, a thing that only happened after a storm, when the air was clear enough to see the mountains.

She was still standing there when Charles came out to her. "Miss Floyd," he said sternly, "you will catch cold in that thin dress. I will fetch the scarf you lent to Janie."

"I am not cold, thank you." She did not turn her head. "The mountains are so beautiful"—

"Admiring the mountains will not keep you warm," he said curtly. The sea was choppy and the boat dipped covering them with spray. "You are getting soaked." He took off his jacket and put it round her. "That will at least protect you from the sea water."

She did not protest. The warmth of his coat on her shoulders gave her the strength to say what had to be said.

"Mr Pitborough," she said steadily. "I have made up my mind to accept your offer. I said I would tell you today, but there has not been an opportunity until now."

"Thank you." His voice was as cold and formal as if he were engaging a clerk for his bank. "I hope you will be happy in your post." But happiness had nothing to do with it. "I will discuss the details with you when you come home."

"That will be best, I think." She matched his coldness with coldness. "I presume the marriage ceremony will take place at a registry office, so that it should not take long, nor involve either of us in a great deal of fuss."

He did not reply and glancing at him she saw him look slightly taken aback. "A registry office?" he repeated. "Is that your wish?"

"Naturally, as I suppose it is yours. We are both very honest people, Mr Pitborough: we must give each other credit for that I think. As the ceremony will be not more than the signing of a contract between us you will not wish for a church wedding any more than I should. There are certain vows to be made in church weddings that in our case would be nothing but hypocrisy." Such vows as "to have and to hold—to love and to cherish."

"Yes," he agreed quietly. "You are right, of course. It shall be as you say. We will consider it when you return."

They were approaching the Riva degli Schiavoni and slipping the jacket from her shoulders she handed it back to him.

"You will be going on with your sister and the

children," she said, "so I will say goodbye, and if I should not see you again before Wednesday I hope you have a good journey home."

Dismissing his thus, she went back into the cabin to help with the disembarkation of the party, while he stayed on deck to summon sufficient gondolas for them all as the boat moved in to the quay.

But through it all his thoughts were occupied almost entirely with Miss Floyd: he found that she chilled him to the bone with the cool common sense that he had found so acceptable at the Palace ball.

14

"You will not desert us?" whispered Rosalind to Cecily as they entered the hotel with Mr Tilverton. "I must have you with me."

"I will be there," Cecily promised her, but she felt slightly apprehensive as she followed the young people upstairs to the private sitting-room hired by Mr Lavender.

Mrs Lavender was sitting by the window quite recovered from her headache. It had passed, she told them, with the storm. "Thunderstorms always have that effect with me, as you know, Rosalind," she said. "They upset me. I hope you did not get soaked? I thought of you all on that exposed island with the little children."

"We managed to find shelter," Rosalind said. "And we also found something else, Barnaby and me. We found that we loved each other, and we want to marry when he is able to support a wife, but in the meantime we want to be engaged." She went over to her mother and knelt down beside her. "Naughty Mamma, to tell such fibs about me being engaged to Mr Ferndean! I never meant to marry him, as you well knew."

Here Barnaby found his voice, addressing the thunderstruck Mr Lavender. "I know, sir, that it must seem to you to be the height of folly for me to consider marrying on my present salary," he said. "But Rosalind and I love each other, and if we have your permission to be engaged I will work as no man ever worked before to make a home for her before many years have passed."

Then Mr Lavender found his voice. "You ask for my permission for my daughter to engage herself for years to a young man with no money and no prospects!" he thundered. "Certainly not. You shall never have any such permission from me, sir, never! I can only wonder at your temerity—your audacity—in suggesting such a thing."

"Papa! Dearest Papa"—Rosalind went to her father and tried to embrace him, but he pushed her away.

"Don't you come 'dearest Papa-ing' me, madam," he said. "I mean what I say. This young man can leave at once, and I will thank him not to see you again before he leaves for England. There is no engagement between you, and there never will be. kindly understand that. Good-day to you, sir!"

Barnaby bowed and without saying any more walked to the door, but Rosalind was there before him, and putting her arms round his neck she kissed him. "We *are* engaged," she said. "Whatever anybody says to the contrary. We are engaged, my darling Barnaby, and when I am of age we will get married. Goodbye, my darling, and God bless you."

The door closed behind him and she went to the window and watched from it until he had gone. Behind her in the room Mrs Lavender turned her reproaches on Cecily. "I did think, Miss Floyd, that you were to be trusted to keep an eye on Rosalind today. The only reason we brought you with us was so that you could prevent anything of this sort happening. You know what Rosalind is like—so impulsive and headstrong. My only comfort is that she usually forgets her favourites quickly enough."

Rosalind turned in time to hear this remark and told her mother vehemently that she would never forget Barnaby. "You had an aunt once," she reminded her, "who was engaged for nineteen years. You told me about her when I was a child. But she married her man in the end, and if I have to be engaged to Barnaby for *twenty* years I shall not take it too badly. If Papa cannot, and Lord Tilverton will not, do anything for him then we shall just have to wait until he is earning enough for us to get married. I don't know what the smallest amount is on which a man can marry, but I daresay it won't be much more than he is earning now, so we shall not have to wait too long." She caught Cecily round the waist and waltzed with her to the door. "Do not look so glum, dearest Cis. If you had tied me to you with your scarf today I would have escaped you!" And she went to her room, singing under her breath.

* * * * *

In the Contessa's great house on the Grand Canal letters were waiting, and among them a solitary telegram from England for her brother. He read the cryptic message it contained with a frown: *"Removal of certain funds needs your urgent attention. Suggest immediate return.* It was signed by his cousin William.

"I hope it is not bad news?" said Miriam.

"I don't know what it is." He showed it to her in silence.

"Removal of funds," she repeated. "Does that mean somebody important has taken his account elsewhere?"

"William would not have sent for me for anything like that," said her brother. "We have lost large accounts before now. No, it is more likely to be a robbery."

"A robbery?" She made a little face. "Somebody has rifled the safe, do you mean?"

"It could be that—but even then I don't see why I should be sent for in such a hurry. We don't keep fortunes in the safe, after all. I suppose William could have found out about some big misappropriation of funds that has been going on for some time, though I doubt it he has the wit for it. But these things do happen and we lost fifty thousand pounds once through a dishonest clerk. Oh well, I'd better get the night train to Milan and lose no more time thinking about it."

"Will you take Janie with you?"

"If Nurse Appleby can get packed in time. I will go to the station at once and book *wagon-lits* for us all."

"Mr Tilverton will accompany you?"

"I would like him to do so. He is a child about travelling, otherwise I would have left him to follow on Wednesday with Nurse and Janie."

Miriam had expected Nurse Appleby to be resolute in not being able to be ready in the two hours that was all that could be allowed for her packing, but the thuunderstorm had set the seal on her dislike for foreign parts.

"Begging your pardon, m'lady, but you never know where you are in these countries," she told her. "No fit water for the children to drink, and milk turning sour under your eyes. I shall be glad to get Miss Janie home to civilized ways again. No offence meant, m'-lady, but it's all according to what you're used to, and don't you worry about us not being ready in time. Please tell Mr Charles as everything will be packed by the time he wants to start." And she set to packing with a will, in which she was helped by Contessa's nurse: Janie was asleep and they left the waking and dressing of her to the end, and just before they left, Nurse Appleby, her bonnet strings all ready tied under her double chin, put a small parcel into Miriam's hand.

"It's Miss Floyd's scarf," she told her. "The one she wrapped round Miss Janie this afternoon. Very nice young lady is Miss Floyd. I saw the master give her his coat on the boat as we was coming back."

"Did he indeed?" Miriam had not observed such gallantry on the part of her brother.

"Ought to get married again, did Mr Charles, m'lady," said Nurse, "Especially now that Miss Pit-borough is leaving us come Michaelmas."

The Contessa had not heard that either, and it made her more thoughtful still, and on the following

Wednesday she asked Cecily and her friend in to entertain her as she and the children felt berefit, she told them, with the two men and little Janie gone.

Mrs Lavender raised no objection: she was as glad to see them go as they were to accept the Contessa's invitation.

"Pitborough showed sense in taking that young man back with him right away," Mr Lavender said when the Contessa's note arrived. "No doubt he told him what had happened and he would not dare to offend me by encouraging him in any nonsense. My account at Pitborough and Orde's Bank is not one that he will want to lose in a hurry. I can only wonder that he has taken such a fancy to the young scamp."

"I think consideration for Mr Tilverton's health made Mr Pitborough decide to bring him with him." Once more Cecily felt impelled to defend the absent Charles. "He had been very ill, Mr Lavender."

"That's as may me, Miss Floyd." Mr Lavender was snubbing. "But I fancy Mr Pitborough is a business man first and last, and I doubt if he will have much to say to Mr Tilverton after he gets him home."

The girls were glad to escape from the hotel for the day. Life was not very happy at that moment, what with Mr Lavender declaring that he had had enough of Venice, and that he had decided to go on to Rome instead of staying out their full time there, while Mrs Lavender treated Cecily to long periods of hurt silence and her daughter to a peevish fault-finding over trifles that was almost as bad.

The Contessa was in the garden of the palazzo with the children and their nurse, and during a pleasant morning in the shade of the trees the girls learned that it was bank business alone that had taken Mr Pitborough and his friend home so suddenly. "Poor Charles," the Contessa said. "They never will leave him alone for long."

After luncheon, however, while Rosalind was turning the pages of a book of views of Venice in the salon, she took Cecily away with her to fetch her scarf, and also to show her a bracelet that she thought Bella might like. "If she is as fond of jewellery as most little girls," she added, "she will like bangles as much as I did when I was her age."

The bracelet was found and gratefully accepted, and put aside with the scarf, and then the Contessa said, "Before we join your friend again, my dear, I want to have a little private conversation with you. My brother told me what his business was in Venice, and about the propositon he made to you. I was horrified and I told him so. I have never minced words with Charles, and we have always been very close to each other. And although I would dearly like him to marry again, I would not like him to marry any girl on the terms he made with you. They are utterly cold-blooded and not fair on you—a fact that for some odd reason seems to have escaped him."

For a moment Cecily was silent and then in a quiet voice, as emotionless as Charles's had been when he had discussed the matter with his sister, she told Miriam that her brother had simply told her the truth. "And I have accepted his terms," she added. "He needs a hostess for his house when his aunt goes back to Gloucestershire, and Janie needs a mamma, and I shall do my best to fulfill such duties as are necessary at Oatesby. I shall be amply rewarded by the generous provision he proposes to make for my family. The ceremony of marriage will simply be a convenient way of stilling scandalous tongues."

The Contessa frowned. "Charles told me that he could not—and indeed would not—become emotionally involved with any woman again," she said slowly. "But he was so determined about it that I almost hoped he was more attracted to you than he cares to admit."

"Oh no. There is no mistake about that." Cecily's reply was quick and decided. "As far as I am concerned I am sure he has nothing but a mild contempt for me—because of the bargain I made with him as to the disposal of my family."

"Ah yes—your family." The Contessa was obviously not happy about that part of it either, and then she asked curiously: "And for yourself? Is it all a matter of business for you too? Have you no affection for Charles either?"

Cecily hesitated. "I'd like to say that it was so," she said then in a low voice. "I never intended to feel anything for him at all. He wanted the whole affair to be a business proposition—very well, I thought, he should have it in his own way, and be done with it. And I may as well tell you at once that when I made that stipulation about my family I never dreamed that I should hear anything more about it. I was astonished—and slightly shocked I think—when he followed me here to Venice to put his plan for my family in front of me. Most men would have taken no for an answer."

"But not Charles. He wouldn't. He enjoys a challenge, you see."

"And that is how he saw it? My concern with my family I mean. As a challenge?" And then as the Contessa remained silent, "It is only since I have seen so much of him here that I have learned to know him better—to appreciate perhaps qualities in him that I did not know existed, and gradually—I don't quite know how—I have come to realize how much he means to me." Cecily looked through the long windows of the Contessa's dressing-room at the great palazzos on the far side of the Canal, and the sparkle on the water was so bright that it hurt her eyes. "That is partly why I have agreed to his absurd—and I suppose, very masculine—bargain, so that I shall at least see him sometimes, living in his house at Oatesby." Her voice shook a little. "I suppose all this sounds very unlikely to you. You must think of me as a designing harpy, anxious to catch a rich man for herself and her family. But it is not so."

"I am thankful for that." The Contessa joined her in the window and took her hand. "If you love him, that is all I want for him, and if I were you I'd take him up on his 'bargain' and I'd see what proximity can do. He will probably fight you every inch of the way, mind. His first marriage was so disastrous that it is understandable that he does not want to run the risk of loving again."

"There was a tragedy, wasn't there? It is said in Milchester that they were on a holiday abroad when his wife died suddenly."

"It was more than that." Miriam hesitated and then she said decidedly, "Yes, it is only right that you, above all people, should know the truth. Gussie was a gay, frivolous little creature, never happy when she was not surrounded by friends of both sexes. She loved admiration—indeed I don't think she could have lived without it. My mother detested her but even she admitted that she had wit and a great deal of charm, and she was very lovely to look at. She sang prettily—though not with your depth of feeling—and one of her favourite songs was the one you sang as an encore at Lady Rand's party."

."Not 'Early One Morning'?"

"Yes, that's the one. And there's no need to look so conscience-stricken. It was not your fault, and Charles was the first to point it out. My brother fell headlong in love with her, and I have thought since that here her parents, who were desperately poor, were as much to blame as anyone, for persuading her into the marriage. She was never in love with Charles: she refused to have children for the first five years of their marriage, and she resented Janie's advent more than she had ever resented anything before. After the child was born she would not have anything to do with it, or with Charles. She said she preferred to live in London, that Oatesby bored her to death. He bought a house for her in Belgravia where she spent money like water, giving parties and balls and entertaining her friends, until one day he had a visit from his father-in-law bringing him a letter that he had received from Gussie telling him that she was leaving her husband for another man, and that they were going to Italy that night. To do the old man justice he was desperately distressed, for Charles as much as for his daughter. My brother followed the couple and caught up with them in Naples, which was at that time in the grip of one of its epidemics of cholera. I don't know what sort of lodgings they were in, but by the time he found them she had caught the disease."

"And—the man?"

"Oh, he had left her. He was afraid of catching it I daresay. It is not a romantic complaint. Charles was with her until the end: she died in his arms."

"Poor Charles!" The name slipped out unconsciously. "It explains so much though. I understand now why he will never want to consider having another wife."

"Never is a long time," said Charles's sister enigmatically.

"He is a determined man," Cecily reminded her sadly. "But thank you for telling me. It will help me a great deal in future." A future that was to be shared—and yet not shared—with Charles Pitborough. And then they rejoined Rosalind.

As they were on their way back to the hotel in one of the Contessa's gondolas Rosalind asked her friend why their hostess had kept her so long.

"We were discussing the prospect of me taking a position in a household that she knows," Cecily said composedly.

"A position?" Rosalind was puzzled and then she thought she knew what her friend meant. "Not as a governess, or anything dreadful like that?" she exclaimed. "Cecily—dearest Cecily—things cannot be quite as bad as that, surely? I mean, to be a governess in an English family would be bad enough, but to be employed as one in an Italian household would be indescribable."

"*Not* a position as a governess, Ros."

"Then are you going to be a companion like old lady Scrim's poor old Miss Bunny? You couldn't be another Miss Bunny, Cis!"

"No. Not as a companion either." Cecily laughed at Rosalind's dismay. "I cannot tell you any more just yet, but you will know in good time. In any case it is a position that I have made up my mind to accept."

"How mysterious you are. Will it help your family?"

"Yes, it will." Cecily was surprised to find that she had scarcely given her family a thought all day, and even now her concern was entirely for Charles Pitborough.

15

When Charles arrived back in Milchester he told his coachman to drop him at the bank before taking Janie and her nurse on to Oatesby. "You can come back for me later," he said.

He found his cousin William and the Senior Partner from Lancashire waiting for him.

"What in the world has happened?" he asked. "From your telegraph William, one might have thought to find the bank in smoking ruins."

"You may well ask what has happened," said his uncle grimly. "Your cousin will tell you."

"I realize that it was my fault," William said unhappily. "I mean, we should have checked the damned things—even if it meant staying all night and coming back on Sunday, whereas now we only have the old man's word for it that the parcel contained two hundred thousand pounds."

"Supposing you start at the beginning?" said Charles, his jaw tightening, and haltingly William told him about the arrival of Sir Matthew Billing on Saturday afternoon, with his absurd brown paper parcel, and how old Summerscales had wanted to stay and check its contents and he had said that Monday would do, and had sealed it himself with the bank seal before it was put away in the safe.

"And when we got here on Monday morning," he concluded, not daring to look at his cousin, "we found that thieves had got into the vaults by a tunnel from the house next door and had broken open the safe and had taken eight hundred pounds in gold and the parcel. The police think that the robbery had been planned from the start, and that the man Turnbull is a professional thief who is wanted in Australia for a series of crimes."

"No doubt he only planned to take gold and notes, though," said Joseph Orde. "The parcel was a gift from heaven—they must have opened it, and seeing the bearer bonds knew that once the alarm was raised they would be more easily disposed of than notes on Pitborough and Orde's Bank. So they took all the available gold and the parcel."

"I suppose the bank will have to make it good?" said William reluctantly, and repeated that they only had Sir Matthew's word for it that the bonds were worth all he said they were.

"As we are responsible for their safe keeping then of course we will make it good," said Charles crisply. "Nobody will argue about that. Fortunately I can— and will—repay the sum out of my private capital."

"The bank——" began his uncle, but Charles cut him short.

"*Not* the bank," he said curtly.

"But are you saying that you can *afford* to lose two hundred thousand pounds?" said his uncle.

"Nobody can afford to lose such a sum," Charles said. "But as it is part of the fortune that my father made—perfectly legitimately—from Orde money, I feel more responsible for repaying it than my Senior Partner." His eyes, cool and slightly mocking, met those of his uncle's and the old man puffed and blew and said not at all, and that he did not see it that way, and gave in grudgingly with the remark that it was good of his nephew to think of it. "I live very quietly at Oatesby," Charles went on, "and my share of the profits from the bank is sufficient for my needs. The only reason why I have liked to keep a large sum in hand is in case a sudden crisis should blow up and there is a run on the bank, although the Bank of England will usually be ready to underwrite a private bank like ours, if its owners can show sufficient security."

The Senior Partner assured him gravely that he would be prepared to use his own capital in such a case, and having learned that the police were to meet him at the bank on the following morning, Charles only waited for the return of the Oatesby carriage to take himself home.

When he had gone William said thoughtfully, "He did not tell us what business it was that took him to Italy."

His uncle smiled rather grimly. "My dear William," he said, "when a man of Charles's age goes abroad on business and will not disclose what it is, it is usual to assume that it has to do with a woman. Under the circumstances I should advise you to follow my example, and ask no questions."

All that the police could tell Charles the following day was that Gerald alias Jake Turnbull might have been involved in another bank robbery earlier in the year in a town in Yorkshire. A man passing himself off as an invalid had taken a house next to a bank, and had actually been pushed out in a bath-chair in the local park by his accomplice, posing as his son-in-law. After the bank had been broken into and the contents of the safe stolen—amounting that time to ten thousand pounds—the invalid and his "son-in-law" disappeared. Like the robbery at Pitborough and Orde's it had been done over a Sunday, so that it would not be discovered until the Monday morning, thus giving the thieves time to get away.

"In these days of rapid travel," the Inspector told Charles wryly, "with fast trains and equally fast steamers to cross the Channel, the men could be on the Continent before the theft was discovered."

And remembering the speed with which he had travelled home from Italy, Charles could only agree.

* * * * *

The robbery was not enlarged upon in the local paper: a certain amount of gold had been taken, it was said, but no valuables, and the loss of Sir Matthew's bonds was not mentioned at all.

By the time Cecily came home a fortnight later it had almost been forgotten, and after a trip made increasingly uncomfortable by Mrs Lavender's coolness, she was thankful when Mr Storey's cab finally deposited her and her luggage at her uncle's door.

She arrived in time for luncheon and the family made much of her while even Mrs Floyd found no fault with the lace scarf that she had brought with her from Venice. It was neither too long, nor too wide, and she did not say once that she never wore white.

Bella's bangle was put on at once and generally admired, the boys' leather pencil cases were taken back to school that afternoon, and the General's quiet thanks for his cigar-case were accompanied by the remark that it was nice to have her home again.

When later on she went upstairs to start unpacking her mother followed her, and seating herself in the small uncomfortable chair by the window she sent the housemaid away, saying that she would help her daughter instead. Once the girl had gone however she made no attempt to move from the chair, and as Cecily went on quietly putting her things away in wardrobe and drawers, she began playing with her rings and bracelets and said how much she had enjoyed her visit to her old friend in Cheltenham.

"I am so glad. How is Aunt Julia?"

"As charming as ever, dear." Mrs Floyd smiled rather self-consciously. "She could not have been kinder to me—or more understanding." She paused a moment and then said with a constraint that was so unlike her that it made her daughter look at her with surprise, "I sent Ellen away because I have something to tell you, Cecily, and I don't quite know how you will take it. I have not told the others—only dear old Humphrey, and he suggested that I should wait until you came home before I broke it to the boys and Bella. The fact is, my dear, that when I was staying in Cheltenham I met a very old friend of your father's—Sir Digby Longbarn. He was so pleased to see me again, and so flattering—he said I did not look a day older since he saw me last in London. And I was so glad to see him too. He lost his wife a few years before your dear papa died, and it was quite like old times. We went for walks together and he accompanied us to concerts and plays in the evenings—Julia was very naughty about him, calling him my "beau"—and the long and the short of it is that on the day before I left Cheltenham he proposed to me and I accepted him."

"Oh, Mamma!" Cecily embraced her mother with more genuine affection than she had felt for some time. "I am so glad for you. When are you going to be married? Have you decided yet?"

"Early in September, my love. Digby wishes the boys and Bella to make their home with us. The boys will go to Cheltenham College, and Bella will have a governess until she is ready to go to the Ladies' College there. That nice Miss Beale is still headmistress and everybody speaks so highly of her." She hesitated and then she said tentatively, "As for you, my love, I feel sure your uncle wishes you to stay on here with him. It would be too cruel to deprive him of us all. He would be very lonely with only the servants for company."

Cecily said quietly that if her uncle would like her to stay on with him, she would be happy to do so. Her mother kissed her effusively.

"I knew it!" she said. "I said so to Digby when we

were discussing my family. 'As for Cecily,' I said, 'I don't think I shall be able to persuade her to leave her uncle. She has been so devoted to him since her father died.' He quite understood. And of course you will come and visit us whenever you like, dearest—that is to say when it is convenient, of course." She left the room, looking back at the door to say triumphantly, "It will be pleasant to be able to take precedence of Lady Scrimgour. She is only the widow of a knight—*I* shall be the wife of a baronet!"

After the door had closed behind her Cecily sat down on the side of her bed for a few minutes to think over what she had heard. It was only too painfully clear that her mother did not want a grown-up daughter with her in Cheltenham. Schoolboy sons and pretty little daughter of ten were welcome, but a gawky girl of twenty-two was a different matter altogether.

She sighed and smiled a little ruefully as she returned to her unpacking, and as she worked she found that she could look forward more than ever now to the bizarre post that had been offered her at Oatesby. No longer was there any need for Charles Pitborough to buy a house for her mother or to settle any money upon her. All such embarrassing projects were at an end. She had only to wait until he called on her uncle and everything would be settled between them. She was beginning to look forward to his visit with an almost painful eagerness, but every morning she looked for a letter that was not there and for a visitor who did not come.

As the days slipped into a week and the prospect of her mother's wedding submerged everything else, the memory of Venice became more and more like a dream, receding into the past, and she wondered if Charles had heard about Mrs Floyd's approaching marriage and had thought better of his own offer to her daughter in consequence. In the meantime there was a great deal to be done: the wedding breakfast was to be held in the General's house, but the ceremony was to be at the Cathedral and taken by the Bishop himself. Every moment of every day in that wet English July was full to the brim and Cecily managed to push the thought of Charles Pitborough into the back of her mind with the memory of sun-drenched Venice. He had never pretended to feel any affection for her, after all, and his aunt might have decided to stay on at Oatesby, and there was no longer any need for her own services there. It did not occur to her that there might be other things on Charles's mind as well.

A few days after he had arrived home Mr Lavender visited the bank and was astonished to see a fair-haired young man among the clerks in the outer office, and upon enquiry was told by Mr Summerscales that he was a new member of the bank's staff.

Mr Lavender returned to his house in a fury and summoning his daughter asked if she knew that young Tilverton as now employed at Pitborough's.

"Oh yes." Rosalind smiled happily at her father. "He has been there ever since they came home. He lodges with Mrs Chadwell, which is so much better for him than those horrid London lodgings."

"And may I ask what princely sum Pitborough is paying him?" demanded Mr Lavender, beside himself with anger to think that his daughter had been taking Bonnie for walks in Love Lane with a great deal of frequency since their own return.

"The same that the government office was paying him in London I believe," said Rosalind.

"Then you will not see him again," said Mr Lavender. "You will give me your promise on that."

"I am sorry, Papa, but I cannot promise any such thing, and unless you lock me up I don't see how you are going to stop me from seeing him. In fact I shall see him as often as I like, because I consider myself to be engaged to him and always will."

"We shall see about that." Mr Lavender rang the bell to order the carriage for that afternoon. "If Pitborough does not want to lose my account he will dismiss that new clerk of his at once and send him back to London."

After a luncheon eaten in stony silence, during which his daughter remained irritatingly serene, he went down to the bank and demanded to see Mr Pitborough on a matter of extreme urgency. Charles received him politely and asked the angry little man to take a seat.

"I shall not sit down and I shall not stay long," said Mr Lavender. "You have young Tilverton working in your office, I see."

"He is one of my clerks. You are quite right." Mr Pitborough was unruffled and his customer felt ready to burst with wrath.

"Perhaps you do not know that the young man has been making love to my daughter, sir?" he said. Mr Pitborough regarded him gravely but with an unaccustomed hint of amusement.

"I don't think you can blame him for that, Mr Lavender. Miss Lavender is a very pretty and a very charming girl."

"And she is not going to be thrown away on that young wastrel," stormed Mr Lavender.

The amusement disappeared from Mr Pitborough's eyes. "I am sorry, Mr Lavender, but I must take exception to that," he said quietly. "Mr Barnaby Tilverton is no wastrel. He is a hard-working good young fellow and I am pleased to have him in our bank."

"Then you will have to dismiss him," stormed Mr Lavender. "Unless you wish to lose my account."

Charles's eyebrows went up but otherwise he did not seem to be concerned. "The bank will be sorry to lose a good customer, Mr Lavender, but my partners and I never allow ourselves to be influenced by monetary considerations when we are convinced that we are doing a thing that is right. I bid you good-day."

"I mean what I say," thundered Mr Lavender.

"I have no doubt you do, sir." And Mr Pitborough sent for Mr Summerscales to show him to the door.

That evening Mr Lavender sat down and wrote a long letter to Lord Tilverton, with the result that early in the morning two days later the Tilverton carriage blocked the way in the High Street for half an hour while his lordship was in Pitborough and Orde's Bank.

As he passed through the outer office on his way to Mr Pitborough's room Lord Tilverton took a hard look at a fair-haired young man who was sitting there bent over a ledger, and not having seen him since he was the age of ten he was somewhat startled to see the likeness to his own father that was imprinted on the young face.

As the door closed behind him and he took the leather armchair that the acting Senior Partner drew forward he came to the point at once.

"I have received a disturbing letter from Mr Lavender in The Crescent," he said. "He tells me that you have a young kinsman of mine employed here—Mr Barnaby Tilverton. I would like to know if it is true?"

"Quite true," said Charles, and waited.

"I took some pains to obtain a post for him in a government office in London, Mr Pitborough," said his lordship haughtily. "I would like to know on whose authority you saw fit to advise him to relinquish it and come here—to be employed by you as a bank clerk?"

The contempt in his voice sent a faint flush to the banker's cheekbones, but he replied quietly: "Mr Tilverton wishes to get married, and the department where he worked could not offer him any hope of promotion for a number of years. I have started him off here at a salary of one hundred pounds a year—ten pounds more than he was earning with his government department—and when he has worked in the bank for three years my partners and I have agreed that we will offer him a junior partnership."

"A partnership?" Mr Pitborough's visitor was evidently put out, although he tried to hide it. "And whose capital do you expect to use for that, Mr Pitborough? I presume he will be obliged to bring some money into your firm, rich as it may be."

"He will work for his capital, Lord Tilverton. At the end of three years, when he should have picked up some notion of how we run things here—and he is no fool—he will then be able to draw four hundred pounds a year, and his share of the bank profits over and above that will accrue for a further five years. We consider that at the end of that time he should be able to put down a sum sufficient for a full partnership in the bank. He seems to think that he will be able to marry on four hundred pounds a year, and I daresay he will when the time comes."

"But—has he an account here?" Barnaby's uncle was frowning now as if he were contemplating something that he did not think about.

"It is not the habit of the bank to divulge its customer's business affairs to other people," said Charles gravely. "But as he is our employee and you are his uncle and I suppose, in that case, might consider yourself to be in some way his guardian, I have no objection to telling you that his account with the bank consists of a small overdraft. I did not want him to run it, but he insisted. He had a bad accident in London in the spring and one of your old servants went up to London and fetched him down to her cottage here and nursed him until he had recovered. Naturally he wished to pay for his keep but government departments do no pay their employees when they are away from work through accident or illness. So reluctantly, I arranged an overdraft for him and although he repaid most of it before he left London he is now repaying what remains by doing some tutoring that the Bishop has found for him in the evenings. He has a number of friends in Milchester, Lord Tilverton, as well as a few enemies. Mr Lavender is among the latter: he has the curious idea that a Tilverton is not good enough for his daughter."

It was now his lordship's turn to flush. He thought it over and then said abruptly, "I would like to see the young man."

"Certainly. I will have him sent to you." Charles

retired to the Senior Partner's room, Joseph Orde having returned to Lancashire, and in a few minutes the young man entered the room where his uncle waited for him, and as he saw him face to face Lord Tilverton again became aware of his likeness to his grandfather.

"Did they tell you who I am?" he asked, not offering to shake hands or even getting up from his chair.

"They said you are Lord Tilverton, so that I suppose you must be my uncle," said Barnaby stiffly. "But as I have not seen you since I was ten years old, when you told me you had arranged for me to enter Christ's Hospital as a pupil, I am afraid I do not remember you in the least."

Was the boy trying to make him angry? If so, he was almost succeeding by the way he looked and spoke. There was no respect in voice or manner, only a certain arrogance. He said curtly:

"I understand that Mr Pitborough and his partners have given you employment here as one of their clerks?"

"That is so."

"It did not occur to you to ask my permission before you terminated the employment that I had obtained for you in London?"

"It did not." Again that assured look, that insolent tone.

"May I ask why?"

"Becuase you have never shown the slightest interest in me either while I was at school or after I had left I naturally concluded that you had washed your hands of me. And I would add, Lord Tilverton, that I prefer it to be so. I do not wish to be held responsible to any man from now on: I am my own master."

Damn the boy, thought his uncle. He was his grandfather over again. In just such a way would the old man speak and put up his head, defying anyone to contradict him. He said more gently: "I am sorry if I have seemed to treat you harshly in the past. But I hated your father who brought ignominy and disgrace on the family time and again. I could not bring myself to feel affection for his son."

As Barnaby did not reply his uncle continued with a return to his former curtness: "Mr Pitborough tells me that you have an overdraft with his bank. I will settle that for you this morning. He will also need several thousands of pounds later on, no doubt, if he and his partners do as they say and take you into partnership. When the time comes I will pay the amount they require into your account."

"I beg your pardon, Lord Tilverton, but you will do no such thing." Barnaby's head went up and anger glinted in his eyes. "I am working off the overdraft myself, with no help from anybody, and I shall do the same later if the bank is good enough to offer me a partnership. I take nothing from anybody—and especially from you."

"You had better take care, sir!" His uncle got up and took up his gloves and cane, ramming his tall hat more firmly on his head. "I shall never offer you anything again."

"I sincerely hope that you will not, sir," said his defiant nephew and showed him in silence to the door. He then went to the Senior Partner's office and told Charles rather ruefully what had transpired. "I do hope he will not move his account from the bank, sir, as Mr Lavender has done," he said. "If he does I feel it will be entirely my fault."

"It will be nobody's fault, Barnaby." The banker rested his hand for a moment on the boy's shoulder with an encouraging pressure. "There are some people who unfortunately seem to think that they can rule others and indulge their own whims simply by the payment of sums of money. They still have to learn that things like honesty and integrity and human feelings cannot be bought. And now go back to your desk, for God's sake, or Summerscales will be giving me black looks for keeping you. He takes his tutoring of newcomers seriously."

16

The following week Lord Tilverton's account was also moved from Pitborough and Orde's, and although when Barnaby heard of it he was abject with contrition, Charles was far more worried about the loss of Sir Matthew Billings's bonds. One afternoon he left William in charge and went over in his dog-cart to visit the old gentleman in his dilapidated mansion at Little Creevey to tell him about the robbery.

He found Sir Matthew in a very good mood. He welcomed him in the smoking room, through a thick haze of tobacco smoke, with a cackle of laughter, and said that he supposed he had come about the parcel he left at the bank.

"Well yes, I have, sir." Charles did not see that it was anything to laugh about.

At that however the old man chuckled so much that he lost his breath and ended up with a fit of coughing

that sent him blue in the face. "Read that letter from
my old sister at Clumpton Hall," he said, throwing it
over to Charles, and then before he could pick it up
he had snatched it back again. "No, you won't be
able to do that. Her writing is like a spider's and I can
only decipher it myself. The long and the short of it
is that she is furious with me, because I sent her the
present I had promised her from Paris after I got
home, and it wasn't what she expected. She says here
—I'll read it to you—'What do you think I want with
a parcel of your dirty bits of paper?' And she sent
it back by the carrier. By the carrier, mark you!" A
fresh fit of laughter ending in coughing nearly finished
him, and when he had recovered he got up and went
to the cupboard by the fireplace, unlocked it and took
from it a badly done-up brown-paper parcel, which he
threw on the table in front of the banker. "Only two
hundred and fifty thousand pounds in bearer bonds,
my dear fellow! Sent by the carrier in that parcel on
one of the wettest days of this confoundly wet summer. It might have burst open at any time." He paused,
watching the expression on Charles's face. "I presume
you did not open the parcel I left with your partner?"

"I had no chance." Charles smiled grimly. "That is
what I came to see you about. It was put into the bank
safe unopened, and that night it was stolen, with all
the available gold we had there."

"Was it by gad?" The old man stared. "Then if
you had not opened it, what did you propose to do
about it?"

"The bank was prepared to refund the value of the
bonds. There was nothing else we could do."

"But you only had my word for it that they were worth all that money."

"We haven't had occasion to doubt your word in the past, Sir Matthew."

"Ye haven't, have ye?" The old man frowned, then he said shrewdly, "But if the thieves did not untie the parcel—and I assure you that if they had they would not have taken it—how did they know that it was supposed to contain these bonds?"

"That I am afraid was due to gullibility and breach of confidence on the part of one of our clerks. The fellow who took the house next door to the bank was an Australian, and promised him a thousand a year in a bank in Sydney, and the wretched man believed him. Turnbull got all the infomation he wanted out of the idiot. He's been severely reprimanded and I think it will be a lesson to him."

"You have not dismissed him then?"

"No. He has been with us for a number of years, and Summerscales seems to think his domestic affairs were not very happy. They may improve now." Charles hesitated and then he said, "Would you mind telling me, sir, exactly what the bank is responsible for? This parcel that we had in our safe—what did it actually contain?"

Another fit of coughing and chuckling threatened and then the old gentleman gasped out, "It contained a dress length of plum-coloured velvet. Would you not have liked to see the thieves' faces when they finally unpacked it?"

Charles agreed that it would have been a sight worth seeing, and he joined Sir Matthew in a brandy to celebrate the safety of the bonds.

*   *   *   *   *

In the meantime Rosalind started to wear an engagement ring at home, threading it on a gold chain under her dress when she went out. It was of turquoise and diamonds and had belonged to Barnaby's mother. Her father's reply to this latest piece of bravado was to summon her brother Jack from London to add his remonstrances to those of her parents. But after having had a talk with his sister he had only been immensely amused by her account of the affair and told his father before he left he had not thought Ros had it in her, and that he advised him to give in.

"She was always a stubborn little monkey under that dutiful air of hers," he added. "And she is quite determined to go through with it."

"I think Mamma is beginning to realize that I mean what I say," Rosalind told her brother when she went to see him off at the railway station. "She was actually looking at a house today—a very small one—in the Close, and reckoning up ways and means. I daresay Papa will come round in time. And in the meantime I shall see Barnaby again this afternoon at Lady Scrimgour's. Isn't Lady Scrim a pet? I met her in the park one day when I was feeling rather low and she asked me what was the matter and I told her, and she wrote and asked me to tea last Saturday to meet some young friends for croquet, and of course Mamma could not say no. And Barnaby was there and it was a fine afternoon for once, and we played croquet together on Lady Scrim's lawn and it was heaven."

It had never occurred to Jack Lavender that croquet on Lady Scrim's lawn could be heaven, but he kissed his sister just as the guard blew his whistle and advised her to make the best of it. "Heaven has a habit of coming out of the clouds once you are married," he told her as the train bore him away.

The first time Cecily heard about the bank robbery was when her uncle happened to remark one morning in the smoking-room that he understood it had not been as large as had been feared.

"But when did it happen?" asked his niece.

"In June sometime—about the time that you were in Venice. They sent for Charles Pitborough and he came home right away."

So that was why he had left so suddenly. Cecily said aloud, "That is probably why he has not been here to see you."

"Been to see me?" The General was surprised. "Why should he have come to see me?"

She flushed a little and then, snatching this rare opportunity when she was alone with her uncle, she told him about Charles's plan for providing for her mother and family and how she accepted it as part of the bargain between them. "He said he would come and see you directly I was home," she said. "But as he did not come I thought he might have heard that Mamma and the family were provided for by her marriage to Sir Digby and thought better of his offer to me, as the provisions I laid down were no longer necessary."

The General walked to the window and back. "And you expect me to believe," he said incredulously, "that Pitborough went to Venice simply to put a business proposal before you? Nonsense, child. The fellow must be in love with you."

"Oh no. There was never any question of that. I told you so before I left with the Lavenders."

"I know you said so at that time. But my dear girl, I refuse to believe that a rich man like Charles Pitborough would have taken the trouble to go all those miles just to ask you to reconsider your refusal of him. I repeat, the fellow is in love."

Cecily shook her head. "Indeed, you are quite wrong. He has never left me in any doubt about that."

"And you?" The General's eyes were uncomfortably shrewd. "Do you care for him?"

"I love him so much," she said simply, "that I'm afraid I would live in his house on any terms he liked to offer me."

"As bad as that, is it?"

"Are you shocked?"

"My dear, nothing shocks me—except perhaps unkindness and cruelty." He put his hand on her shoulder and let it rest there tenderly. "And has he always been cold to you? Have there never been moments in that romantic city of Venice when you might have thought that he cared?"

Her mind went back to one magical moment in Florian's Restaurant when they sat over ices at one of the little tables there, and he had told her that she would not find him an unreasonable man and just for one second their eyes had met. And what had the Contessa said about her brother? That he would fight her every inch of the way because he could not run the risk of loving anyone again. "I don't know," she said slowly. "There have been times when I have thought

that he—might think more of me than he allowed himself—and me—to believe. When I once suggested that
he should look for another girl in Milchester he said
that—I was the only one who would do. But he had
always been so correct—so formal—so cold."

"Then I think it is time that you came to some con-
clusion one way or the other." The General kissed her
affectionately. "I want to go and see Fullerton this
afternoon about a mare he has that might take my
weight if I start hunting again this winter. I've got a
lot heavier over the past few years. His place is only
two miles beyond Oatesby, and as it is a Saturday Pitborough will probably be home early from the bank.
I'll send a note down to him to tell him that I will be
calling on him during the afternoon. I shall not mention the fact that you will be with me."

"Me? But, Uncle Hump—you don't want me to be
there—"

"It is essential that you should be here. Don't look
so dismayed, my dear." He was firm about it. "Put on
one of those pretty dresses of yours—it looks as if we
are having one of our lovely warm summer days for a
change. I'll tell Pringle to have the gig ready at three."

The note was despatched and a polite reply came
from Mr Charles Pitborough that he would be pleased
to see the General at Oatesby at four o'clock, and at
luncheon Cecily's uncle remarked that he was taking
her out with him that afternoon.

Mrs Floyd protested. "I cannot spare her, Humphrey. Miss Kemp is coming to fit me with some of
my dresses this afternoon and I depend on Cecily to
advise me—"

"Then I am afraid you will have to do without her

today. She has been kept too busy with your dresses lately and I want to bring some colour into her cheeks." The General dismissed his sister and her dressmaker.

When the gig was brought round Cecily was ready for it. She had taken trouble over her appearance, her uncle noticed with approval. A light alpaca coat was thrown over the voile dress in buttercup yellow that she had worn that afternoon at Florian's, and a small hat in golden straw was perched on her head. But when the gig eventually left her outside the big house at Oatesby, it needed all her courage to pull the bell and give her name to the butler. "I shall be back in an hour," the General had told her. "Pray give Mr Pitborough my compliments and tell him that when you see him."

The butler took her coat and parasol as she entered Oatesby for the first time. She gripped her gloved hands together tightly and followed him across the great hall with its wide staircase and the gallery above: she had the feeling that it was welcoming her and yet at the same time holding aloof, that the ladies who had been its mistresses in the past were watching her critically from the shadows. An employee like herself might be accepted as part of the household, she thought sadly, but as part of the family that owned it, never.

Charles Pitborough was seated at a writing table in the library with a pile of correspondence in front of him, writing a letter, and from the contents of a waste-paper basket beside him it looked as if he might be finding it difficult. As she was announced he looked up quickly and then got slowly to his feet.

"Miss Floyd," he said, and then, "I was expecting your uncle."

"I am the bearer of his apologies," she said, giving him her hand in a formal handshake. "He had to see Major Fullerton about a mare he is interested in buying, but he will be with you in an hour. In the meantime I thought that you and I might discuss the business contract that we are planning for Michaelmas. I was sorry to hear about the robbery of the bank: I suppose that is why you did not come to see my uncle after I got home?"

She was pleased that she was able to keep her voice unemotional and cool, and that her hands had stopped trembling.

"That was not the only reason," he said. He drew out a chair for her and went to the fireplace and stood with his back to the great carved stone fireplace looking down at her thoughtfully. "The robbery was not as bad as we had feared, and in any case that would not have kept me away from your uncle. But I had heard that your mother was marrying again and that she was taking her family with her to Cheltenham, and I imagined that you would no longer wish to be a partner in the contract we had discussed. It was one made by you entirely on your family's behalf after all. I was writing to you just now to tell you that I would not hold you to it."

Cecily's eyes went for a moment to the bulging waste-paper basket. "I think you are under a misunderstanding," she said crisply, out to fight him now as his sister had suggested. "My mother is marrying Sir Digby Longbarn in September and at the end of that month my two brothers and my sister will make their home with them in Cheltenham. But I have not been invited to that home—nor would I go. Therefore I think I must hold you to your bargain, Mr Pitborough." She took off her gloves and laid them on the arm of her chair: it was a very warm day. "I do not know where the Registry Office in Milchester is situated but I shall be ready to meet you there at whatever time suits you in October, and move into my rooms here afterwards."

His expression did not change: his eyes were resting on her as thoughtfully as before, and she wondered if she had failed. "Unless," she said carefully, "you have changed your mind?"

"No," he said. "I have had no reason to do that."

"Then shall we get down to business?" She kept her voice steady. "Would it not be a good idea if I were to see your housekeeper before my uncle arrives and discuss with her the rooms I am to have here? I would like to see them, so that I may know if there is room for anything I would like to bring with me."

For a moment he looked a trifle embarrassed. "I am afraid I have not told her yet of what we intend to do," He hesitated and then he said quietly: "Would you mind very much if we had a church ceremony?"

She was so startled that she did not know what to say. "A—church ceremony?" she repeated slowly.

"Yes. You see, my people here will rather expect it, and there's my aunt—and others. It needn't be a long affair—it could take place in Oatesby church here if you have no objection."

She could not answer. Crowding into her mind came the thought that he had sworn to that other girl to have and to hold, to love and to cherish, in sickness and in health, till death did them part. And she laughed at his devotion, was utterly faithless, and died in his arms. Pity and love for him undermined her coolness and her careful formality: her throat constricted and her eyes filled with tears. He saw them and came to her quickly, contrite.

"I'm sorry," he said, sitting down beside her. "I've said something to hurt you—"

"No," she said, trying to smile. "I'm just being silly. And I don't seem able to find my handkerchief."

"Have this one." He took a handkerchief from his pocket and she wiped her eyes and then, looking at what he had given her with the initials in the corner so carefully worked, found her tears drying in surprise. "Why," she said, "this is mine. I lost it that morning when I was sketching on Lady Rand's balcony."

"Yes." He was like a schoolboy found out. "I found it after you had taken the things from me at the hotel that morning. I kept it, meaning to return it, and then —because I wanted to keep something of yours I suppose—I did not give it back. I don't know what old Rigby thought about it, but every evening it has been taken from the pocket of whatever suit I've been wearing and put out in the dressing-room with the clean handkerchief for the following morning. He never mentions it and neither do I, but as one can't keep secrets from Rigby I'm afraid that he knows as well as I do that I am in love with you." He got up and walked over to the windows and looked out rather blindly at the terraced gardens of Oatesby, with their late summer wealth of flowers. "I've been so arrogant and so —stupid—that I know I've made it impossible for you to care for me, Cecily. But perhaps in time"—

She got up quickly and joined him in the window. How could she ever fight him? "You made it difficult, Charles," she agreed gently, "But not impossible."

He swung round and the smile that had always troubled him was trembling on her expressive mouth, and the moment at Florian's was back with them again. "Do you mind removing your hat?" he said unsteadily. "It is very fetching but there is a wicked pin in it and I don't want to lose an eye."

"Why?" The smile became a laugh: he really was a most unexpected sort of person. "What are you going to do?"

"Take off your hat, woman," he said. "And I will show you."

She took off her hat.

17

Miss Pitborough, impatient with the General for not having arrived, sent a footman to tell his master that tea was ready. "I shall not wait for General Masterson," she said.

The lad, new to his job, disappeared and in a few minutes returned, looking considerably startled.

"Well?" she said sharply. "Did you tell your master that tea was ready?"

"Please, miss—ma'am, I did tell him, but I don't think he heard me."

"Nonsense! Why did he not hear you?"

"Please, miss—ma'am, there is a young lady with him."

"A young lady?" Miss Pitborough rose majestically. "In that case I will go and tell him myself." As he held the door open for her she paused eyeing him severly. " 'Miss' is correct, and 'ma'am' is correct—but 'miss-ma'am'—never!"

She went on to the library and stopped short in the doorway. Charles was seated in a deep armchair with his back to her and on his knee with her arms clasped round his neck and her head comfortably settled on his shoulder, was Miss Floyd.

Miss Pitborough walked round to the front of them and was there for at least a minute before they saw her. Then Cecily slipped off Charles's knee and picked up her hat from the floor, blushing violently. Charles was not in the least put out.

"Well, Aunt Hannah," he said composedly, "I have taken your advice and found myself a wife."

"And about time too," she said. She congratulated him and gave Cecily a hairy kiss. "As for you, my dear, you little know what you are taking on, but I will say this for Charles, he is not an unreasonable man."

"I have told her that already," Charles said. He waited while Cecily put on her hat and then he took her left hand and slipped his own signet ring on the third finger. "Just to make sure of you," he said.

They followed Miss Pitborough into the small drawing-room as she said it was cosier for tea, and although the apartment must have measured thirty foot by forty somehow it was a very cosy tea party that gathered there, especially when they were joined by the General, who said at once that he would not wish the couple happiness because it was written in their faces.

And afterwards Janie was brought down to meet her future Mamma, which she did with delight, her pleasure being echoed by Nurse Appleby later on as she talked over the engagement in the housekeeper's room after Janie was in bed.

"I thought something was in the wind when we went off to Venice in all that hurry," she said, pulling up her skirt to warm her knees by the housekeeper's fire, because the evenings were chilly in that old house. "Nasty, wet place Venice. It can't be good for anybody to live in the middle of all that water. All them boats— and the smell of the canals, Mrs Bolingbroke, has to be endured to be believed—and not a cab to be seen anywhere. Not Christian, really, living like that."

"I must say Miss Floyd seems a nice young lady," said Mrs Bolingbroke. She had liked the way she had shaken hands with her and said she hoped she would be at Oatesby many more years to help and advise her. Not like Mrs Wilbur Goldmeyer, who was always complaining that the water in the bathroom was not hot. With all those miles of pipes to go through from the time it left the boiler to the time it arrived in the tap was there any wonder that it wouldn't be hot any longer? Much better to have hot water taken round to the dressing-rooms in the old-fashioned way, and baths set out in front of nice warm fires like they'd always been at Oatesby until Mr Charles's mother married her American husband.

And Miss Floyd wasn't like the first Mrs Charles either, spoilt little hussy that she was.

"I think," said Mrs Bolingbroke, looking up at the large, yellowing photograph in its frame over her chimney-piece—a photograph that portrayed Charles's father with his four-in-hand and Charles as a little boy, sitting proudly on the box beside him. "I think

Miss Floyd will suit Oatesby very well."

It was left to the Contessa to express the family's feelings later in a short and delighted telegraph message from Italy: "Bless you both, Miriam."

When Mrs Floyd saw the signet ring on Cecily's hand at dinner that night she was rather put out, although her brother remarked that he thought Sir Digby might be pleased at the thought of having a rich banker in the family.

"But fancy giving her his signet ring!" said Mrs Floyd.

"I am only to wear it until he changes it for a wedding ring," Cecily told her.

"I never heard of such meanness," said Mrs Floyd. "I am afraid, dear, their may be some truth after all in the rumours that are going round about Pitborough and Orde's Bank. It must be in a *very* bad way if Charles Pitborough cannot give his future wife a proper engagement ring."

After dinner, however, she did manage to elicit from her daughter that Charles intended to have some of the family jewels reset for her. "But not now, Mamma. Later on."

"Well, *that* won't cost him much." said her mother. "Sir Digby thought *me* worthy of the best ring that money could buy!" She spread out her left hand and the diamonds flashed in the lamplight. "He chose the stones himself at Asprey's."

But Cecily only smiled.

"And when do you propose to get married?" asked her mother peevishly.

"At Michaelmas. You will be back from your wedding trip by then and the boys and Bella will be with you in Cheltenham."

"But who will make your wedding-dress? Not Miss Kemp surely?"

"I am not having a wedding-dress, Mamma."

"No wedding-dress!" Horror rendered Mrs Floyd speechless and Cecily seized the opportunity to explain.

"We worked it all out over tea, did we not, Uncle Hump? Uncle will drive me out there one morning early, and we shall be married at Oatesby church with Uncle to give me away, and I shall wear a travelling dress, because we shall leave at once for London. It won't be a long wedding-trip like yours—only from Saturday to Monday, because Charles will have to be back in the bank on Monday."

"I never *heard* of such a thing." Her mother was shocked. "A hole and corner affair if ever there was one, and I don't think Sir Digby will like it at all. My poor child, what have you done in becoming engaged to such a man? No engagement ring, no wedding-dress, and no proper wedding—"

"Indeed it will be a proper wedding, Mamma. I will show you the marriage lines afterwards if you like."

"Do not be vulgar, Cecily. And then no honeymoon. Where will you go on Monday?"

"Home to Oatesby," said her daughter radiantly.

"It is almost indecent," complained Mrs Floyd, and then, as Cecily laughed, "I don't know what's come over you, but it was that visit to Venice that brought it all about, I'm sure of that."

"I daresay you are not far wrong there," said the

General, winking at his niece as he made for his smoking-room and the comfort of a cigar.

"Venice," said Cecily, with a light in her eyes that was like a reflection of the dancing water on the painted ceiling of Lady Rand's balcony, "is a *most* romantic city!"

Romantic Fiction

If you like novels of passion and daring adventure that take you to the very heart of human drama, these are the books for you.

☐ AFTER—Anderson	Q2279	1.50
☐ THE DANCE OF LOVE—Dodson	23110-0	1.75
☐ A GIFT OF ONYX—Kettle	23206-9	1.50
☐ TARA'S HEALING—Giles	23012-0	1.50
☐ THE TROIKA BELLE—Morris	23013-9	1.75
☐ THE DEFIANT DESIRE—Klem	13741-4	1.75
☐ LOVE'S TRIUMPHANT HEART—Ashton	13771-6	1.75
☐ MAJORCA—Dodson	13740-6	1.75

Buy them at your local bookstores or use this handy coupon for ordering: